Jealous: The Bitch That Has My Man

By: Kellz Kimberly

D1521291

Text **KKP** to **22828** for Updates, Spoilers, Giveaways, Announcements, & So Much More!!!!!

Chapter One

April 2015 Three Months Earlier

"Julani!!!!" I heard my father calling my name but I was too tired to get out of bed. I let him call me three more times before I finally rolled out of my bed. I slipped my feet into my hello kitty slippers and made my way downstairs to where my father was.

"Yes Dad." I said once I was in front of him.

"What are you still doing sleep. It's one in the afternoon; I told you I needed those pickups down by three." He scolded me.

"Daddy I was getting ready to get dressed and head out before you called me." I lied.

"Don't lie to my face Julani! You might be able to run game on these little ass niggas but you can't run that shit on me. Now go upstairs get dressed and go pick up that money." My father said and walked away.

I rolled my eyes and took my ass upstairs to get dressed. My father was the one and only King Cortez. He was the main drug supplier in Brooklyn; there were two things that he didn't play with, me and his money. My father didn't want me to be one of those spoiled females that had everything handed to her so he made me work for what I wanted. He never let me touch any drugs or know what was going on within the camp but he did make sure I picked up all his money. I was basically his accountant. I handled all his money for him and made sure that it came back clean.

I hurried to get in the shower before my father had a chance to call me again. I quickly washed up, dried off and lotioned my body. Looking in my closet I had numerous choices of things that I could wear but it still felt like I didn't have anything. It was the third week of April and spring was just starting to get into effect. It wasn't cold outside but it wasn't all that nice outside either; New York always had some crazy ass weather. I decided on my black Nike leggings and my all black Nike hoodie. I slipped my feet into my Bred 11's threw my curly hair into a ponytail and was out the door before my father could say anything else. I climbed into my black Mercedes Benz CLA 250 put my bag on the passenger seat and pulled out the drive way. I was ready to hurry up and pick up my father's money, drop it off and then start my day.

*****

By six I finished all my picks up except for one and I saved this one for last on purpose. I pulled into Messiah's drive way applied an extra coat of lip gloss and got out the car. I walked over to the door knocked twice before the door opened and the man of my dreams was standing in front of it.

"Juju wassup?" Messiah said calling me by my child hood nickname.

"You know same old same old." I said starring at him with lust in my eyes.

Messiah had been my crush ever since I was 14. He was 18 at the time and just started working for my father. My father took him under his wing when Messiah came to him asking him to front him some work. Messiah grew up going from foster home to foster home and didn't have anyone to look out for him leaving him to look out for himself. My father was impressed with how Messiah stepped to him so he put him on and basically raised him as his own. Now at the age of 25 Messiah was getting money left and right. Even though my father raised Messiah as his son I didn't look at him in a brotherly way, he was way to fine for that. Messiah had a sun kissed brown skin complexion with the most beautiful dark brown eyes I had ever seen. His hair was cut close in a cesar but his waves were still on swim. He stood at 6'3 and had a body that looked like it was sculpted by god himself.

"Julani I know you not day dreaming again." Messiah said snapping his fingers in my face.

"Boy if you don't stop that shit." I said laughing.

"You always got your head up in the clouds girl." He said licking his lips.

I had to bite my tongue because the next set of words that I was going to say was going to get me in trouble.

"Don't worry about me, where your girl at?" I asked just to be nosey.

"She out shopping you know doing what y'all females do."

"Uh huh don't put me in the same category as her because the type of female I am goes shopping with her own money and saves her nigga's money for a rainy day." I smirked putting him up on game.

"Well what nigga's money you putting up for a rainy day your father's? I never see you with a dude." He said bursting my bubble.

"Don't worry about me just focus on your little girl friend."

"You don't have anything smart to say now do you?" he asked staring at me with those beautiful brown eyes.

"Trust me I always have something smart to say I just rather keep it to myself."

"Yea ight let me get you this money so you can go about your business." He said walking off.

I watched him as he walked away and I couldn't help but to feel jealous of Amara. She had something that I definitely wanted and she was the only thing standing in the way. From what I knew Amara had been with Messiah ever since they were 16. They met in one of the foster homes that Messiah was staying and when he left she left right behind him. The two of them seemed unbreakable and it pissed me off because she was the only thing that was stopping me from getting my man. Messiah and I would flirt from time to time but it was harmless, please believe if he ever gave me the chance I would put it on him in a heartbeat. I wasn't a home wrecka or anything like that but for Messiah I would be. In my defense though they had been together for nine years and there was still no ring on her finger or a bun in her oven so something had to be wrong.

"Here." Messiah said getting my attention.

I took the duffle bag out his hand and threw it over my shoulder. I didn't bother counting it because Messiah always came correct.

"Thank you very much and you're coming to my birthday party right?" I asked as I made my way to the door.

"When is it again?"

"The 23rd" I said with a little attitude.

"I know when it is so stop with that little attitude and of course I'm coming, you know I have to show love to the little sis." He said causing a frown to appear on my face.

"Thank bro." I said sarcastically and walked out the house.

I walked to my car popped the trunk and put my duffle bag inside. I got in the car peeled off and drove the short distance to my house. I pulled into the drive way took everything out my car and went straight up to my bedroom. Messiah calling me sis had me in my feelings just a little. I didn't understand what was so special about Amara that she was the chosen one. Yea she was pretty but if you asked me she didn't have anything on me.

Who ever said light skin was the right skin had never met me. I had a rich chocolate skin complexion that was as smooth as a baby's bottom. I was 5'9 and had never ending legs. I wasn't one of those big booty chicks with boobs that didn't fit their body but I had just enough curves that kept a nigga interested and guessing. I had big brown eyes that were chinky in the corner giving me a sort of exotic look. Thanks to my parents Cape Verdean roots I had thick curly hair that reached the middle of my back. I was a show stopper the only problem was that I had everyone stopping except Messiah.

Runnin' through the 6 with my woes, countin' money you know how it goes. Pray the real live forever man, pray the fakes get exposed. I want that Ferrari then I swerve. I want that Bugatti just to hurt. I aint rockin' my jewelry that's on purpose. Niggas want my spot and don't deserve it. I don't like how serious they take themselves. I've always been me I guess I know myself. Shakiness man I don't have no time for that. My city too turnt up I'll take the fine for that.

Drake's song 'Know Yourself' started playing and I began rapping along. I thought someone outside was blasting music but when the same verse kept playing I realized it was my phone. I looked all through my bag trying to answer my phone before it went to voicemail.

"Hello." I said when I finally found it.

"Wassup chicka what you doing?" My best friend Phallyn asked

"Nothing I just got done running some errands for my father."

"Well get dressed and come get me because I'm trying to go out tonight."

"Phallyn you always trying to go out somewhere. When do you ever stay your ass home?" I questioned laughing.

"I'll stay home when I get a man. Until then I'm gonna have fun in someone's club." Phallyn said laughing but I knew she was dead ass serious.

"You are crazy but you know my father don't like me in these clubs like that."

"I know which is why we not going to a club we're going to the car show they're having out in the heights."

"Now you know I'm not even trying to go over there. Them nigga's don't have any sense."

"It's not even going to be like that. Please just come with me you know you're my only friend." Phallyn begged.

"Fine Phallyn but as soon as some shit pops off I'm leaving whether you're with me or not." I told her.

"Damn Julani you just going to leave a bitch out there?" Phallyn questioned.

"You damn right because I don't want to go there in the first place." I told her.

"Well I'll be damn I thought we were closer than that." Phallyn laughed.

"You know you my bitch but when those bullets fly they don't have a name on them." I told her speaking straight facts.

"I hear you Juju I still love you." She said laughing

"Yea I love you too so be ready I'll be there in the next three hours or so. I have to clean up before I get dressed and leave."

"Ight just call when you're on your away." Phallyn said and hung up the phone.

Phallyn and I had been best friends since our freshman year in high school. We were the complete opposite but we made it work. Phallyn was pretty as hell so I never had to worry about her being jealous when it came to our friendship. Her skin complexion was high yellow and she had beautiful grey eyes that had every nigga calling her ass foreign. She was 5'4 and built like a brick house she had ass and tits for days. She was the Ivory to my Ebony and I would do anything for her just like I knew that she would do anything for me.

I emptied all the money out the bags on to my bed and started separating it into bands. This would be the only way that I was going to be able to clean it up. I always split the money into three different groups. There was a group that would go to the bank, then another that would go in the safe at the club my father owned and the third would be put into stocks and bonds. With the amount of money my father was bringing in I always made sure that not too much went to one place. It was my job to protect my father and his money because my father was all I had left. My mother passed away while giving birth to me and I always felt like it was my fault. I felt like I owed my father something because of my mother's death which is why whatever he asked me to do I did it with no questions asked.

I finished dividing and wrapping the money and put it all under my closets floor board. It's was too late to be traveling with all that money, I figured I would just drop everything off tomorrow as soon as I woke up. I freshened up before putting on my bandeau bra with my leather jumper. I didn't know if I wanted to put on heel's or throw on some Jays. Either one would have complemented my outfit but I choose my black 4 inch Balmain booties. I sprayed Rihanna's Nude perfume grabbed my bag and went downstairs so I could tell my father I was going out for the night.

"Juju where you going." My father said as soon as I hit the kitchen entrance.

"I'm going out with Phallyn I was just about to tell you that I was leaving."

"I asked you where you were going not who you were going out with."

"I'm going to the car show that's over in the heights." I said avoiding eye contact.

"Julani you know I don't want you over there."

"I know daddy but everyone is going to be there including all the dudes that work for you."

"I don't care who is going to be there, I really don't want you going."

"But daddy I'm 20 and I turn 21 in two days, I'm grown I should be able to come and go as I please." I whined

"I know how old you are Julani and you're right you are grown. So go ahead. All I ask is that you be careful and pay attention to your surroundings."

"Of course I will daddy. I'll see you later don't wait up." I told him and gave him a kiss on his cheek. I was a proud daddy's girl but sometime he was just over protective for no reason. I jumped in my car and called up Phallyn to let her know I was on my way.

"Wassup Julani please tell me you are on your way." Phallyn said answering the phone.

"Yes Phallyn I'm on my way so be ready to go when I pull up." I told her.

"You ain't said nothing but a word" she said and hung up the phone.

I shook my head at her because she was really something else. I popped in Nicki's Pink Print CD and started play Feeling Myself. Tonight it was going to be all about me, fuck Messiah and his bitch because if he didn't want me then that was his loss.

Chapter Two

"Girl you see all these cars out here?" Phallyn asked a little too excited.

"Stop acting like a damn groupie." I laughed

"I'm not acting like a groupie shit I'm 21 I'm just trying to meet someone worth my time."

"I feel you there" I told her shaking my head.

"You need to be out here looking for someone too and leave Messiah old ass alone."

"Messiah's not old he is only four years older than us."

"I don't mean old as in age I mean old like he's tired he's old news. That nigga got a bitch that he's not leaving no time soon and from the looks of it she's not leaving him either. So you need to get out that high school crush phase and find someone that's going to pay you as much attention as you pay him." Phallyn said speaking nothing but the truth.

"Girl shut up and bring your ass on." I said stepping out the car.

"You can tell me to shut up all you want but that's only because you know that what I'm saying is the truth." She said getting out the car behind me.

"I know what you're saying is the truth and I respect it but tonight all I want to do is party and have fun. I don't even want to think about Messiah." I told her.

"Well you might not want to think about Messiah but he's right there with his bitch." Phallyn said nodding her head to the right.

I turned to look and there Messiah was standing next to Amara I rolled my eyes at the both of them and turned my head.

"Come on and let's go get a drink." I said

"You don't have to tell me twice." Phallyn said.

We strutted across the parking lot like it was our own personal run way. We went over to the bar that they had set up and ordered two long island ice teas. Once we got our drinks we strutted right back across the parking lot and sat on the hood of my car. A couple of dudes came over and tried to talk to me but I wasn't interested in any of them. I kept stealing glances at Messiah and Amara. Just the sight of them laughing and smiling in each other's face was making me sick but I couldn't stop looking and wishing that was me.

"Why is such a pretty girl sitting over here and looking so mean" A dude said walking up to me with his friend.

"This is just my face." I replied to him his approach caught me off guard just a little.

"I highly doubt it but what's your name ma." Dude said to me. By now his friend was all in Phallyn's face. I took a minute to look at dude he was cute I couldn't deny that. Standing in front of me was a six foot chocolate Adonis. His dark hair brought out the waves so good that I started to feel a little sea sick. He didn't have anything on Messiah but he did have it going on.

"I'm Julani but you can call me Juju and your name is?" I asked back

"I'm Cree." He said looking me up and down

"Cree" I said "That's an interesting name."

"It's an interesting name for an interesting person." He smirked.

"Well tell me just how interesting you are." I flirted.

Out the corner of my eye I saw Messiah walking towards me so I rubbed Cree's arm just a little.

"Wassup Juju and Phallyn?" Messiah asked once he got to where we were.

"Nothing chilling." Phallyn said before turning her attention back to the dude she was talking to.

I didn't even bother replying I just continued to talk to Cree like Messiah wasn't there.

"Now tell me what is so interesting about you." I said to Cree again.

"Julani you going to act like you don't see me standing here" Messiah said.

"What do you want Messiah I'm trying to have a conversation." I said with an attitude.

"You already know what I want don't act like we not people's." He said eyeing me. Then he turned his attention towards Cree. "Wassup man I'm Messiah"

"Cree" Cree replied keeping it simple.

"Look if you need me I'll be over there, be safe Juju." Messiah said sizing Cree up.

"Yea but I'm pretty sure you have someone else that you have to keep safe." I said

"I don't know who you're talking about." he said smirking and playing dumb.

"I'm sure you don't but you will know pretty soon because here she comes now." I mumbled.

"Julani hey girl I didn't know you were here" Amara said giving me a hug.

"Yea I came with Phallyn." I responded dryly.

"Oh okay well y'all have fun. Come on baby I'm ready to go." She said talking to Messiah.

"Ight. Juju I'll catch you on the flip side ma." Messiah said.

"Bye" I waved.

"Who was that an ex or something?' Cree asked once Messiah and Amara were out of ear shot.

"Nah he just a family friend" I told Cree

"Oh ight but how 'bout we go get breakfast and get to know each other a little better?" He suggested.

"I got one better I'm tired and I have to get up early tomorrow to handle business. So why don't you give me your number and I call you when I'm ready to cash in my rain check." I said handing him my phone.

"You better call me too Juju." Cree said handing me back my phone.

"Don't worry I got you." I told him

"Jacori we out my nigga." He said to his friend.

His friend whispered something to Phallyn causing her to start giggling and then the two walked away.

"You just had to cock block didn't you" Phallyn said getting off the hood of my car.

"No one was cock blocking I'm just ready to go and since I'm your ride that means you're ready to go too." I told her getting off the hood and getting in the front seat.

"You're such a buzz kill. Did you not see how fine Jacori was?" She said fanning herself.

"Yea I did but you need to calm down and stop acting like you pressed for dick." I told her pulling off.

"Bitch I am pressed for dick we all can't be like you." She smirked

"What's that supposed to mean?"

"It means that you don't seem phased by sex. The last time you had sex that I know of was maybe like a year ago when you was dating that dude that was from Bedstuy. I don't know how you went a whole year without it but girl I could never." Phallyn said being her normal dramatic self.

"Don't get me wrong I love sex but I find sex more pleasing when you do it with someone that you're connecting with. I don't want casual sex I want intimacy."

"Different strokes for different folks" Phallyn said shrugging her shoulders.

I left the conversation at that because there was no need to go any further with the situation. The rest of the ride was a silent one and I was okay with that. I dropped Phallyn off and told her that I would talk to her later on in the day. By the time I pulled into my drive way it was two in the morning. I walked in and went straight for my bed all I wanted to do was sleep for the next ten hours. Before I called it a night I plugged my phone into the charger and put my phone on silent. I noticed I had a text message, I opened it and too my surprise it was from Messiah.

Messiah

You looked good tonight Julani but you almost got dude fucked up.

I looked at the text confused as hell, what the hell was Messiah talking about. I was tempted to reply but I left the situation alone. I was too tired to play these games with him. I put my phone on the nightstand cuddled up with a pillow underneath the covers and took my ass to sleep.

Chapter Three

I didn't wake up until three in the afternoon the next morning. I yawned and attempted to get out of bed but my head was pounding. I said fuck it and decided to stay in bed a little bit longer. I turned the TV on and started flicking through channels looking for something to watch; I settled on watching Law & Order SVU. I picked up my phone to check and see if I had any missed calls or texts. The only thing I had was a message from Phallyn telling me to call when I woke up. I went back to the message that Messiah sent me and decided to find out what he was talking about. I sent him a text with about six questions marks. I sat my phone down and nervously waited for him to text me back. It felt like time stopped moving as I kept checking my phone to see if Messiah had finally sent a text back.

After twenty minutes of waiting for Messiah to text me I said forget it and sent Cree a good afternoon text. Unlike Messiah he sent me a text right back asking me what I was doing for the day. I told him that I had a couple of stops I had to make and then I would be free to do whatever. I was waiting for a text back from him but instead I got a phone call.

"Hello" I said answering the phone.

"Yea that texting thing was starting to get boring I would rather hear your voice."

"Well now you can" I giggled.

"Since your busy now, how about we go out to Buffalo Wild Wings once you're done with all the running around that you have to do?" He asked

"I'm down with that, Buffalo Wild Wings is one of my favorite places to go." I told him.

"Cool, I'm in the middle of something right now but text me when you're done handling your business and we'll link up."

"Okay" I said and hung up the phone

I started thinking about what Phallyn said about finding someone that was going to pay me the same amount of attention that I show them. Messiah had a girl already and from the looks of it he wasn't paying me any mind. Phallyn was right I needed to get out of this high school girl crush phase and find someone that was worthy of my time.

*****

I had just finished dropping all my father's money off and was ready to go meet up with Cree. When I called to tell him that I was ready he told me that he would be there in about thirty minutes. Since I was closer I knew that I would get there first. I sat in my car waiting for Cree when my phone vibrated I looked down and saw that it was Phallyn calling me.

"Hey bitch wassup." I said greeting Phallyn on the phone.

"You didn't get my text?"

"Yea my bad I didn't wake up until three in the afternoon."

"Your ass always sleeping late."

"I know. If I didn't know better I would think that I was pregnant."

"You have to have sex to get pregnant" Phallyn said laughing.

"Yeah whatever but what you doing?" I asked her

"About to go meet up with dude that I met last night."

"That's crazy." I said laughing. "I'm waiting for Cree now."

"Let me find out you finally taking my advice."

"I had no choice too. Messiah sent me a drunk text last night talking about how good I looked and how I almost got Cree fucked up."

"Say word." Phallyn said

"Word bitch Word. I sent him a text with question marks but his ass never replied."

"Y'all two are funny." Phallyn said laughing.

"It's not me it's his dumbass. I'm telling you he doesn't want to be with Amara because if he did he would have been put a ring on her finger."

"For real because I would never be with a dude for nine years and not have a ring on my finger." Phallyn said agreeing with me.

While I was on the phone with Phallyn my phone made a noise letting me know that I had a text message. I looked at it real quick and saw that it was Cree telling me that he was inside already.

"Phallyn I'm gonna have to let you go, Cree just sent me a text saying he's here."

"Ight girl have fun and let me know what happens."

"You already know I'm going to call you as soon as he and I go our separate ways."

"Oh are we getting ready for the party tomorrow at your house right?"

"Yea make sure you at the crib by nine because I'm leaving at ten."

"Don't worry I'll be there earlier than that because we going to pre-game.

"Ight but let me get off this phone." I told her and hung up.

I got out my car and made my way to the entrance, it didn't take me long to find Cree because my eyes automatically landed on him.

As soon as I looked at him our eyes locked. I walked over to him never breaking our eye contact.

"Hey." I said once I was close enough to him.

"Wassup beautiful." He said pulling me into an embrace.

I blushed a little as I pulled out of the hug. "Are you ready to go inside and eat because I'm starving? I asked.

"Yea I already got us a table." He said taking my hand and leading the way. Once we sat down at our table the waitress came over and took our order and said she would be right back with our drinks.

There was this awkward silence between us as we sat at the table waiting for our food. I was hoping that this wasn't going to be one of those dates that lacked conversation because I didn't have a problem with just getting up and leaving.

"Why you over there looking nervous. I don't bite ma not unless you want me too." He smiled.

"I'm not nervous I just hate sitting in silence." I told him

"So get to talking ma."

"How about you tell me what makes you so interesting?"

"We still on that I see." He laughed

"Yea we are so you going to answer it or Nah."

"I'm not like other dudes ma and that makes me interesting."

"What do you mean you're not like other dudes?" I asked truly interested

"You will just have to keep fucking with me to find out. But tell me about yourself Julani. Tell me your likes and dislikes, tell me what turns you on and what turns you off." He said looking at me with lust filled eyes.

"You just get straight to the point don't you?" I said.

"I don't beat around the bush when it comes to something I want." He smirked.

The waitress came back over with our drinks and wings. I started eating my wings while thinking about what Cree had just said. I wasn't sure if I was going to answer his questions but it did feel good to be wanted. Not a lot of dudes tried to talk to me because of my father; whenever I would try to introduce my father to someone he would nip it in the bud real quick.

"Cree what do you do for a living?" I asked him

"That's none of your business." He replied simply.

"Mhmm we going to take that route I see. Well if you don't want to tell me who you are I'll let you know who I am."

"Okay." He said laughing.

"I'm Julani Cortez the daughter of King Cortez." I smirked.

"Was that supposed to scare me ma because it doesn't. Yea I know who your father is and I respect him but like I said before I know what I want and when I want something I usual get it."

"So you don't care that once I introduce you to my father everything will be over and done with between us if he doesn't like you?" I asked with an eye brow raised.

"How old are you Julani?"

"I turn 21 tomorrow."

"You a grown ass woman and still letting your daddy control who you date. I can only see you doing that for one reason."

"Oh really and what reason would that be."

"All the dudes that you bring to your father you really don't want to fuck with which is why you introduce them to your dad. Your dad does your dirty work for you and I can bet that the nigga you really want is the dude from the other night." He said reading me like a book.

"If he is the one I want then why am I sitting here with you?"

"You can't have him because another chick got him. So you're using me for something to do when there's nothing to do." He shrugged.

"And you're okay with that?'

"I'm okay with it for the mean time because trust and believe, I will be the nigga you want soon enough. Now eat those wings before I eat them for you." He said and went right back to eating.

I watched as he ate his wings and he had my full attention. It was something about what he had just said that made me want to fuck with him. If he didn't mind being my distraction then hell I didn't mind either.

I finished eating the little bit of food that I had left and I was ready to go and get into something. I wasn't going to be the one to offer but if he tried to push up on me I wasn't going to push him away. I needed to live a little and stop putting my life on hold for someone who wasn't thinking about me. After Cree paid the bill we walked out to the parking lot so I could get in my car.

"Did you have a good time?' Cree asked when we reached my car.

"Yea it was cool." I said leaning up against my car.

"It was just cool?" He asked moving into my personal space.

"Yea it was cool." I said.

His lips were inches away from mine and I had the urge to fill the little bit of space that was in between them. Our eyes were locked on each other as if we were trying to see the other person's soul. I decided to make the bold move and fill that space. Our lips met and it was like sparks were flying, a simple kiss led to tongue sucking and hands roaming. We were in the parking lot leaned up against my car having an all-out make out session.

I broke our kiss only because I heard my phone going off in my back pocket. Before I could get it Cree reached and grabbed it for me and showed me the name that was flashing on the screen.

"Your boy calling you." Cree smirked handing me my phone.

"Uh yea." I said looking at the phone trying to figure out if I should answer it or not.

"Girl go ahead and answer the damn phone. I'll catch up with you later." He said kissing me on the forehead and walking away.

I got in my car and watched as Cree walked away from me not even once looking back in my direction. I let out a sigh before I answered my phone "What!" I said not giving a fuck about how rude I was being.

"Julani?" Messiah questioned.

"You did call my phone didn't you?"

"What the hell is your fucking problem?" He said catching on to my attitude.

"Nothing Messiah I'm just tired." I said softening my tone a bit. "How can I help you?"

"I need you to meet me at the crib." He said

"Whose crib?" I asked confused.

"Mines?"

"You sure that's a good idea with how late it is?"

"If you worried about Amara she's not home. Are you going to come through or not?"

"Yea I'ma come through." I told him and hung up the phone.

I pulled out of the parking lot ready to find out just exactly what Messiah wanted to talk about. If I said I wasn't excited I would have been lying. I drove to his house with multiple scenarios of what was going to happen once I got there. I got to his house in forty minutes flat; I was nervous as hell as I walked to the door and knocked. I knocked four times before Messiah came to the door. He was dressed in only basketball shorts, it wasn't Friday but the way his eggplant was poking out you would have thought it was.

"You gonna come inside or what." He said pulling me out of my perverted thoughts.

"Yea sure." I said walking in.

"Why you acting like you never been to my house before?" Messiah asked.

I had been to Messiah's house numerous times but this time felt different. I didn't know whether I should sit down or stand up. I followed Messiah into the living room and had a seat across from him.

"So wassup Juju you got something to tell me."

"No do you have something to tell me." I asked right back.

"You the one running around with a nigga from Harlem."

"Wait what?" I asked confused. This is what he called me over here to talk to you about."

"You heard what I said. Why you fucking with that nigga yo?"

"I don't have to explain myself to you Messiah; you are not my man nor are you my daddy."

"You're right I'm not your man or your daddy but I thought we were fam."

"What is that supposed to mean?" I questioned

"You supposed to be loyal to your fam. Don't act like you don't know."

"Nigga the only one that got beef with them Harlem niggas is you and that's because they bruised your little ego. The only fam I got is my father and Phallyn and you can believe that they got my loyalty." I said jumping out my seat. The fact that Messiah was questioning my loyalty because I was talking to a nigga was pissing me off.

"Julani you not fucking with a nigga anymore is that what you saying?" He asked getting in my face.

The tension that was in the room was thick as shit. One thing about me is that I didn't back down from anyone. Messiah was ice grilling me and I was giving him that same look back, I wasn't one of these little dudes that worked for him he wasn't going to scare me that easily.

"That is exactly what I'm saying Messiah. I don't fuck with you." I told him with venom dripping from my voice.

What he did next shocked the hell out of me; he gripped the shit out of my chin and forced me to kiss him. At first I tried to fight but when he forced his tongue into my mouth and I tasted mint on his tongue I melted.

"What the fuck is this shit!" I heard someone yell behind us.

We pulled apart quick and turned around to see Amara standing in the door way.

"Messiah I'll catch you later." I told him wiping my lip gloss off his lip and then walking to the door. I tried to walk around Amara but she pushed me back.

"Bitch you think you just going to kiss my fucking man, wipe your stank ass lip gloss off his lip and then just walk the fuck up out of here." She said pointing her finger all in my face.

"Messiah you better get her before I do." I said looking back at Messiah.

"Amara sit down somewhere before you hurt yourself." Messiah said causing me to smirk at her.

"Messiah you must got me really fucked up." Amara said

She was still talking shit and pointing her fingers getting rowdy. I knew I wasn't going to make it out of this house until I beat her ass. I started taking off my earrings when Amara caught me slipping and hit me with a two piece. I stumbled a little but regained my footing and hit her with a right hook. We were going blow for blow holding our own until Messiah came over and picked Amara up.

"Messiah you better put me down before I beat your ass too!" she yelled kicking her legs frantically.

"Amara you acting up over a fucking little ass kiss that didn't mean a damn thing." He said

Hearing him say that broke my heart, I didn't even bother saying anything as I walked out the door with tears in my eyes. I got in my car and drove home with tears running down my face and snot coming down my nose. When I pulled into my drive way I sat in my car for a little bit replaying what had just happened fifteen minutes ago.

I couldn't believe that he said the kiss meant nothing to him when it meant everything to me. I knew he had to feel the same way I was feeling because if he didn't he would have never kissed me in the first place. I wiped my eyes and blew my nose making sure that there were no signs that I was crying because I didn't want my father to start asking questions. I walked into the house and there my father was sitting on the couch.

"Hey Juju where you coming from." He asked turning the TV down.

"I went out with a friend to get some wings." I told him. I walked over to the couch and snuggled up against him.

"Everything alright?" He asked me wrapping his arm around me.

"Yea everything is fine." I replied.

"You ready for your party tomorrow?"

"Yes. I have been waiting for this ever since I was 16." I said forcing a smile to spread across my face.

"We 'bout to do it big. I still can't believe my baby girl is grown up." he said kissing me on my forehead.

"I know huh." I said ending the conversation.

I laid on the couch with my head on my father's chest silently crying. Even though I was about to be considered a grown woman in a couple of hours, I felt like a 16 year old girl that had just got rejected by her high school crush.

Chapter Four

The first half of my birthday flew bye, I woke up ate breakfast with my father and now I was out and about to get my nails done with Phallyn. We were in the nail salon and I was catching her up on everything that happened on my date and how things ended with Messiah.

"I can't believe you wiped the lip gloss off his lips while Amara was standing there." Phallyn said laughing.

"I don't care about that bitch she aint nobody. If you ask me she is just a temporary."

"She been temporary for the last nine years I guess huh."

"Phallyn shut up. But for real I don't see her as a threat. I look at it this way if I wanted Messiah I could have him." I didn't tell her what he had said about the kiss because that was a shot to my ego. When I woke up this morning I made a promise to myself to never tell anyone about it and leave it in the past.

"So why don't you have him because you and I both know that you want him."

"You know how I feel about rejection. I have been dropping hints for a minute now but his ass just to slow to pick them up. But yesterday when he kissed me I felt something there. I just need him to make that first move so I know what it is." I told her honestly speaking.

"I feel you there because rejection is a bitch, but what you going to do about Cree?"

"I don't know. He already knows that I have feelings for Messiah and doesn't mind being temporary or so he says."

"Well he can be temporary but I'm thinking about making Jacori permanent." She giggled.

"Wassup with y'all two?" I asked her wanting to be nosy. I was tired of talking about myself and my fucked up situations.

"Girl, yesterday he told me that he just wanted to chill and shit so I invited him over to my crib. Long story short one thing lead to another and when I say this nigga is blessed, lord have mercy and forgive me for my sins but that nigga is BLESSED." She said putting emphasis on the word blessed.

"You so nasty always giving it up." I laughed.

"Aint no shame in my game." She laughed.

"I hear that, you going to bring him to my party?"

"Yeah I invited him. You should invite Cree so he has someone to rock with." Phallyn suggested.

"Good idea I'ma text him now." I pulled out my phone with my free hand and sent Cree a quick text inviting him my party that I was having at Allure night club. When I looked up from finishing my text I saw Amara walking through the door with some bougie looking chick. We locked eyes and I gave her a stank look before turning away.

"There go your brother wife." Phallyn laughed.

"Phallyn shut up before I pop you." I laughed with her.

I didn't know what Amara was doing here but if she tried anything I wouldn't hesitant to pop her ass real quick.

"I hope she don't start no shit, I don't want to have to fuck up my nails." Phallyn said

"I was just thinking that same thing." I told her.

We finished up our nails without any issues besides Amara ice grilling me. I didn't pay it any mind because today was my day and I wasn't going to let Amara evil stare bother me. We were getting up ready to leave when out of nowhere Amara started talking all extra loud.

"Yea I had to lay that bitch out, I walked up in the house and she was kissing all on Messiah."

"What was Messiah doing girl" Her friend said instigating.

"Messiah was pushing her ass away. When she wouldn't get off of him I had to hit her with that two piece combo. You know I don't play bout my man, me and him have been rocking for the past nine years. I'm not going to let some spoiled bitch fuck that up." Amara said laughing and giving her friend a high five.

I looked over at Phallyn and the look on her face let me know she was ready for whatever.

"It's funny how she say she been rocking with him for nine years but she doesn't have a ring yet." I said to Phallyn but loud enough for Amara to hear.

"He must not like it too much." Phallyn said causing the both of us to burst out laughing.

"If you have something to say then say it no need to throw subs." Amara said

"Isn't that the pot calling the kettle black? Oh and before you try and out your business about what happened last night get your facts straight."

"My facts are straight Messiah told me everything." Amara said rolling her eyes.

"You need to get your own man and stop trying to get with hers." Her friend chimed in.

"Bitch mind your business because I'm telling you now that you don't want these problems." Phallyn said.

"Last night I didn't kiss Messiah he kissed me. If you were on your job instead of spending his money then you wouldn't have to worry about another bitch kissing your man. Now if you don't mind I have to get ready for my party that the all of Brooklyn is coming out too."

"Bitch fuck you and that party. You lucky I'm not coming and shutting that shit down."

"You couldn't shut shit down if you tried you must've forgot who I am." I told her.

"Let me tell you something." She said getting up out of her chair. "I don't give a fuck who you are. Your daddy is the one that holds weight in these streets not you."

"And my daddy is also the one that can make you or break you. Play with me if you want too but I promise you if you do I'ma show you how to really shut shit down." I looked her up and down and could see that she was getting pissed off because her face started turning red. I was about to walk out the door when I remembered that her ass snuck me last night.

"Oh and this is for that sneak shit you did last night." I said while punching her in her face.

The first punch I hit her with knocked her down and I jumped right on her throwing blow after blow.

"You better get your ass off her" I heard her friend say.

After that I didn't hear anything else I assumed Phallyn had jumped on her ass. By now the shop was going crazy. Everyone in there was either cheering me on or recording the shit, I was positive that I was going to end up on world star hip hop. I was taking out all my anger and frustration out on Amara when something clicked. I'm over here beating her ass over a man that's not even mine. I slowly got off of her and went over to Phallyn to get her off of Amara's friend.

"Phallyn let's go this bitch ain't worth us going to jail." I said looking at the ladies in the shop help Amara off the floor.

"You go now!" The Chinese lady yelled at Phallyn and me.

I looked at Amara one last time before I walked out the nail salon.

"That bitch fucked up my nail?" Phallyn complained as we walked to the car.

"I can't believe all that shit that hoe talked." I said

"I thought you were going to kill her ass for a minute." Phallyn said getting in the car.

"I had to pull myself together real quick. I can't be out here in these streets fighting over a nigga that's not mine. Especially one that is going to lie about the shit that happened between the two of us."

"I hear that, I don't know what her friend thought she was going to do but she should have known better." Phallyn laughed.

"I heard her say something and then next thing I knew she got real quiet. I already knew that you had jumped on that ass."

"You damn right! I'm not going to just let some bitch jump you."

"And that's why I love you. Now let's go get these nails fixed at the place down the block." I told her.

After the shit that happened at the nail salon I was over it. All I wanted to do was get my nails fixed get dressed, enjoy my part y and get wasted; and getting wasted was exactly what I was going to do.

*****.

"Bitch you killing them in that dress." Phallyn said as we stepped out the limo. I had on a black lace dress made by Givenchy that left little to the imagination. On my feet I had on a pair of Black Giuseppe stilettos with gold accents. My curly hair was in full affect and looking wild.

"Stop it because you acting like you're not dressed to kill, shit you giving me a run for my money." I told Phallyn. She was dressed in a white Balmain dress with Nude Christian Louboutin pumps. Her hair was flat ironed bone straight with a part in the middle. I didn't even have to see what any other chick was wearing in the club to know that we were the best dressed chicks there.

We walked into Allure like it was our own personal runaway, all eyes were on us and that is just how we liked it.

"Oh shit, the birthday girl just arrived y'all! Move out the way so Julani can make her way to V.I.P. Happy Birthday baby girl this one's for you!" The DJ said over the mic.

The DJ started playing 50 cent's in the club and I was ready to go and hit the dance floor instead of going to V.I.P.

"Don't even start we going to go up to V.I.P take a couple of shots and then we can hit the dance floor." Phallyn said.

I laughed at her because she was always on point; I guess that just proved how close we were. It was like she knew my thoughts before I could even speak them. Phallyn and I had to literally push our way through the crowd because everyone was trying to tell me happy birthday and give me a hug.

"Happy Birthday beautiful." Someone said to the right of me. I looked in that direction and saw Cree's handsome face smiling at me. His eyes were low and kind of lazy looking but he made that shit look sexy.

"Thank you boo." I told him giving him a hug and kissing him on the cheek.

I grabbed his hand and led him into V.I.P with me and Phallyn. Phallyn had spotted Jacori and brought him too. Before I sat down I made my rounds saying hi to everyone and thanking them for coming. A lot of the guys that were up there worked for my father and handed me envelops of cash as my present. I thank them all and stuffed it deep into my bag. I was at the end of the line saying hi to everyone when Messiah popped out of nowhere.

"Happy Birthday Juju." He said taking my hand and twirling me around before giving me a hug. "You look beautiful." He whispered in my ear.

"Thank you" I told him and pushed him away.

"Why you acting like that Julani?" He asked pouting like his feelings were hurt.

"You already know why but if you don't mind I'm going to go back to my guest and enjoy my party." I told him and walked away. After what happened earlier and finding out that Messiah lied to Amara about what really happened I didn't have anything to say to him.

I made my way back over to where Phallyn and the guys were at and saw them making idle chit chat.

"What y'all talking about?" I asked sitting down next to Cree.

"Nothing really Cree was just telling me how he would like to rip that dress off of you a little later." Phallyn giggled.

"Oh really is that what you said?" I asked looking at Cree.

"I didn't say all that but shit I wouldn't mind tho." He said looking at me with lust filled eyes. There was no denying the sexual chemistry that was between us.

"Who knows what the night will bring I just might let you do that." I said flirtatiously.

"Ight that's enough of all that flirting shit let's take shots in honor of the birthday girl." Phallyn said. She waved the waitress over and ordered 12 shots three for all of us. When the waitress brought them over she picked one up and stood up to make a speech.

"I just want to say Happy Birthday to my best friend. Julani you are annoying as hell sometimes but I wouldn't trade your ass for anything in this world. I've known you for the past eight years and you haven't changed not one bit. You are still the same old cocky bitch. What I'm trying to say is that I love you girl and let's turn up and turn out." She said raising her shot.

We all followed her lead and lifted up our shot glasses and then threw them back. The first one went down smooth, but by the time I made it to the third one my throat was burning.

"Ahh that shit burns" I said sucking on the lime that was on the side of one of my glasses.

"I got something else you can suck on later tonight." Cree whispered in my ear.

"Boy if you don't get out of here with that nasty shit." I giggled pushing him away.

Since I was a light weight when it came to drinking it didn't take long for me to feel them three shots; I wouldn't say I was drunk but I was definitely feeling a little tipsy.

I know you got all dressed up for the club. Waiting on them to come pick you up. Baby when I saw ya walking out the door I just knew ya needed something more. Now whip it straight back to the crib. Finna give you something that you won't forget. Baby, I just wanna get you out them clothes. I just wanna see you dance in slow motion.

The DJ started playing Slow Motion by Trey Songz and I damn near jumped out my dress.

"This is my song" I said getting up and whining my body

"Juju let's go show these bitches how it's done." Phallyn said getting up and grabbing Jacori hand and leading him out the V.I.P section. I grabbed Cree's hand and followed Phallyn. On the way out I passed Messiah and he was ice grilling me, I wrapped Cree's arm around me and pulled him closer as we walked down the stairs just to make Messiah mad. If he wanted to play this cat and mouse game then I was going to make sure I was the winner.

"The birthday girl done made her way to floor. All you chicks with raggedy weave and ten dollar dresses better move out the way because baby girl bout to show y'all how its' done." The DJ said.

I walked on to the dance floor put my hand up and moved it in a circular motion letting the DJ know to play Slow Motion back. He started it over and I made sure to stand in a way that I was facing the V.I.P section. I started whining and grinding all on Cree keeping it simple until Trey hit that high note talking about he wanted me to dance in slow motion, that's when I started doing the damn thing. I bent over and started jiggling my ass one cheek at time in slow motion before I dipped it low and brung it back up slow. When I lifted my head up my eyes connected with Messiah's. The emotions in his eye showed he was hurt but I didn't give a fuck, I had that same look in my eyes when he said that the kiss didn't mean anything to him.

"Ayo, Ayo Julani you better cut that shit out." I heard my father on the Mic. I looked up and he was in the DJ booth. "Nah on a serious note I just want to say happy birthday to my baby girl and I wish you many more. Oh and by the way Allure is now yours, you have shown me that you have what it takes to handle your own business. Now make me proud and enjoy the rest of you night because you deserve it." My father said before exiting the DJ booth.

"I'll be right back." I told Cree.

I made my way over to where my father was and gave him the biggest hug that I could. "I love you daddy and thank you for everything." I told him

"I love you more and there is no need to thank me you deserve the world and one day you will find someone that is willing to give you that. Now go have fun and enjoy the rest of your party. I'll see you when you get home." He said kissing me on my forehead and walking away. I went back on the dance floor and danced the rest of the night away with Phallyn, Cree, and Jacori.

It was around four in the morning when the party started to whine down and people started to leave.

"Ma you coming home with me tonight." Cree asked leaning up against the wall.

"Yea I'm gonna roll with you but I'm letting you know right now we ain't doing nothing." I told him.

"No one said that we had too. Jacori rolled with me so I'ma drop him off and then you can meet me at my crib." He said caressing my face.

"Okay, let me go find Phallyn and make sure she straight. Text me your address though." I told him about to walk away.

"Hold up ma give me a kiss before you go." He said pulling me back by my hand. I leaned in and gave him a quick kiss. "That's all a nigga get?"

"Yea ." I simply replied.

"Ight you lucky it's your birthday I'ma let you get away with that." He said.

I smiled at him and put a little extra switch in walk just for him. I was looking around the club but couldn't find Phallyn anywhere. I went outside to see if she was there and instead of finding her I ended up running into Messiah.

"Juju" He said

I ignored him calling me and went to walk back inside when he called me again.

"Julani I know you hear me calling you. I don't care if it is your fucking birthday I will embarrass your ass out here." He said.

"Messiah what the fuck do you want?" I asked and turned back around annoyed.

"Drop that bass out of your voice. Wassup with you yo?"

"What's up with me no what's up with you? I'm pretty sure that you know that I beat your girls' ass today in the nail salon."

"Yea I heard, what I'm trying to figure out tho is why you did it?"

"I did it because your bitch tried to clown me and say that I was pushing up on you. I was pushing up on you Messiah? I wonder where she got that idea from."

"You mad because I told her that you kissed me."

"No I don't care that you lied to that girl, what I'm mad about is the fact that you said the kiss didn't mean anything to you.

You didn't feel a thing when we kissed Messiah?" I asked looking him in the eye.

By now the whole club was outside in the parking lot. Messiah was still standing there looking like he was stuck on stupider and it started to piss me off.

"You don't even have to say anything your silence says everything that I needed to know." I told him ready to walk away.

"Julani stop being so dramatic damn." He said letting out a deep sigh.

"I'm not being dramatic I'm being real. I love you Messiah, I have loved your ass since I was sixteen and you were twenty. But your ass was too blind to see that shit and I'm over it now." I told him hurt that he still didn't answer my question.

"You over it Julani you don't love me no more?"

"No I don't fucking love you, and what do you care for when you have Amara's ass at home." I told him and walked away. I was pissed off that he really had me out here on my birthday all in my fucking feelings. I was walking fast hell when I felt someone yank the shit out of my arm. Messiah pulled me into an embrace and kissed me. But this kiss wasn't like the kiss that we shared the day before this kiss was deeper and with a lot more passion.

"I love you Julani." He said ending the kiss.

I didn't know what to think or feel at that moment because he had said what I always wanted to hear. But I couldn't let him get off that easy. I lifted my hand to wipe the lip gloss off his lip but instead of wiping it I smacked the shit out of him.

"That's for having me out here looking like a fucking fool playing with your ass." I told him.

"Juju watch your fucking hands I don't play that shit. Now let's go." He said grabbing my hand.

"What do you mean let's go I have to go find Phallyn and tell her I'm leaving." I told him

"Send her a text and tell her that you are leaving with me." He said.

I did as I was told and sent her a quick text telling her that I loved her and that I would call her later on in the day. Messiah and I hoped in his car and drove out of the parking lot giving a couple of people enough gossip to talk about when my party was discussed. I didn't know where Messiah was taking me but honestly it didn't even matter. All I cared about was that I finally got what I wanted which was Messiah. I looked over at him as he whipped the car in and out of traffic and smiled.

"What you smiling at me for?" Messiah asked looking out the corner of his eye.

"Nothing. Where are you taking me?' I asked him

"Don't worry about it just sit back and relax" he said resting his hand on my thigh.

"I hope you know that you going to have to get rid of Amara."

"I told you I love you right?"

"Yea so." I said

"Ight so that means I got you. I'm not trying to hurt you Juju. I'll handle the Amara thing tomorrow."

I didn't say anything because there wasn't anything left to say. I was going to enjoy this moment and wait to see if he got rid of the bitch. I didn't see anything wrong with going after Messiah because he was supposed to be mine in the first place, but I did see something wrong with me being the side chick. I didn't play that shit, I wasn't going to be anyone's side chick; it was going to either be about me and me only or this nigga could kiss my ass.

"We are here." Messiah said distracted me from my thoughts.

"What are we doing at the Trump in SoHo?" If he thought he was just going to bring me to a hotel and fuck me then he had another thing coming.

"Just come on." He said taking me by the hand and leading me inside.

He walked up to the concierge said a couple of things and then we went to the elevator. I looked around the hotel and had to admit that it was nice. At least he didn't bring me to a damn Holiday Inn. Once we got to our floor we stepped off the elevator and just stood in the hall way for a second.

"Here put this on." Messiah said handing me a blind fold.

"Uh I don't think so." I snatched the key card out his hand and started walking towards our room.

I found our room swiped the key card and was taken aback by what I saw. Walking into the room there were red and white rose petals starting from the door and going further into the room. The room looked like it was a mini apartment and rose petals were all over it. I followed them into the bedroom to find the room lit by candles. On the bed there was a big ass teddy bear that looked like it was bigger than me. The teddy bear was holding a bouquet of roses with a necklace hanging from it. I walked up to the bear took the necklace from around its neck and broke down crying.

For my fifth birthday my dad gave me a heart necklace but he told me that my mom had picked it out for me when she was eight months pregnant. I loved this necklace so much that I wore it everywhere I went. When I was in the fourth grade I got into a fight with this girl over the necklace and she snatched it off ran in the bathroom and flushed it down the toilet. Needless to say I beat that little bitch's ass. The necklace that I was holding was the same exact one that my father had gave me. I looked over at Messiah as he stood in the door way.

"How did you know about this, I didn't even know you when I lost this necklace?" I said wiping the tears from my eyes.

"Your father told me that story when we were talking about gifts for you."

"I can't believe you did all this for me." I said looking around the room.

"Why wouldn't I, Julani I had a thing for you ever since the day I met you when you were fourteen. I was eighteen and trying to make a name for myself and prove to your father that I could handle this business. I didn't have time to try and talk to the boss's daughter, and on top of that I had Amara with me. What Amara and I have is complicated, at one point. I did love her she held me down when I first got started." He said

"You don't even have to explain. All that matters is that we are here now." I told him

He grabbed me by the waist and pulled me into him kissing me. I broke the kiss and lifted his shirt over his head. While locking eyes with him I slowly bent down and unbuttoned his pants pulling them down with his boxers. I helped him step out of them and slowly started to come back up but stopped at his penis. I took it into my small hand and twirled my tongue around the head making him grow instantly. Messiah was indeed blessed with length but he also had thickness on his side. I let his dick go and stood up, I unzipped the side of my dress and let fall to the ground. Messiah picked me up and threw me on the bed. He crawled in between my legs while looking me in my eyes. The intensity that was in his eye scared me just a little but I wasn't going to back down.

He started off licking the inside of my thigh. It didn't take much for him to get a soft moan out of me. The nibbling turned to biting my inner thigh and I lost it.

"Relax Julani I got you ma." Messiah said.

I relaxed a bit and let him continue doing his thing. The bites started to get a little rougher as he made his way up to my love nest. He used his fingers to separate my pussy lips, stuck his tongue and licked clit. When I say this nigga licked everything he licked everything. He started from my opening and finished at my clit. He wrapped his lips around my clit and started sucking slow and then picked up the pace. I was on cloud nine as Messiah slurped up my juices that started to flow. He made sure that he licked up everything and left me completely dry before he eased his body on top of mine

"You sure you wanna do this?" He asked while playing with my opening.

The words "I wanted to" wouldn't form, leaving me to just nod my head. With one quick movement he filled me up causing me to gasp. I wasn't a virgin but I never had someone that was above average. It took me a couple of seconds to get use to the feeling. Once I did my hips started moving in sync with his.

"Ahhhh" I moaned as he bit my neck.

He was giving me long deep strokes hitting my spot with each thrust.

"Juju I love you ma." He whispered in my ear.

I didn't reply I slightly pushed him off of me and laid him back so I could straddle him.

"What you doing ma?" He asked as I lowered myself on him.

I slowly started rocking my hips back and forth. Tonight I just wanted to give Messiah my all. When I was done with him he wouldn't ever be able to question my love for him.

"Bounce that ass for me." Messiah groaned.

I did as I was told and bounced my ass on his dick. Every time I would come down on him he would lift his pelvis up causing his dick to go in deeper.

"Juju." Messiah called out.

"Yeaaaa" I moaned

"Cum for me ma. I want to feel your pussy tighten as your cum flows down my dick." I did as I was told. I bounced on his dick faster and harder, losing all control as my leg started to shake. I felt him tighten around me holding my waist tighter as he was about to cum. I couldn't hold it any longer as I exploded all over him. Seconds later he was right behind me as we both faded in to sinful bliss.

Chapter Five

Two Months Later

"Messiah I don't know what the hell is going on but I'm going to need you to stop dodging my calls" I said pissed off and hung up the phone.

"I don't even know why you are wasting your time calling him. It's obvious that he just wanted some pussy." Phallyn said

"I don't need you to play captain obvious Phallyn." I told her

"Don't get mad at me because I'm keeping it a buck with you. If I was to sugar coat it what type of friend would I be?" she asked leaving my office.

It had been two months since everything went down between Messiah and me. We left the hotel the following morning with plans to meet up later. Messiah was supposed to tell Amara that he didn't want to be with her anymore and I was going to talk to Cree. I guess I was the only one that was serious about it because Messiah never met up with me later that night.

I called him numerous times but not once did he pick up his phone. To say my ego was bruised was an understatement. This nigga really played me for some pussy. Even though it was obvious that pussy is the only thing Messiah wanted I still had hope that it wasn't the case. I sat in the office staring at my phone looking like a sad puppy when Phallyn walked in the room with Jacori and Cree. I was surprised as hell to see Cree because the last time we talked I told him that I didn't want anything to do with him and that we couldn't even be friends.

"Look who I found outside of the club." Phallyn said in a high pitched voice.

I just stared at her as she pulled up chairs for Cree and Jacori. The look on her face confirmed what I already knew; she had set this whole shit up.

"What brings you guys to Allure so early in the day?" I asked just to be polite and make conversation.

"We just wanted to see what you've done with the place since you took over." Jacori said.

"I didn't change much I wanted to keep everything the same. The only thing I redid was the V.I.P section." I told Jacori.

"That's wassup." Jacori said nodding his head.

Cree never said a word he just kept looking at me like he was trying to stare into my soul. This whole gathering was awkward for me and Phallyn was to blame.

"Phallyn what was your point in doing this?" I asked

"You need to get out of this slump that you're in Juju. Before shit popped off with you and Messiah, you were really feeling Cree." Phallyn

"I appreciate what you're trying to do Phallyn but this just isn't the time. I am trying to make sure that this club is up and running for the party that's tonight. I honestly don't need any more stress from another nigga." I said.

"Give us a minute." Cree demanded

Jacori got up and left while Phallyn hesitated to get out of her seat. I nodded my head letting her know it was okay to leave. Once she walked out the door Cree got up, closed it, and made sure it was locked. He had been quiet this whole time and now he wanted to talk, I leaned back in my chair kicked my feet up on my desk and waited for him to say whatever it was that he needed to say.

"Julani you're not as tough as you think you are you know that." He said while pushing my feet off the desk.

"I never said that I was tough."

"You might not have said it but you damn sure act like you are. You put up this front that nothing bothers you or gets too you when all it takes is someone you love hurting you."

"Cree what the hell are you talking about?" I asked

"As soon as Messiah showed your ass a little interest you just jumped all on the nigga forgetting that he had a chick."

"I didn't forget that he had a chick I just don't care about the bitch."

"You might not care about her but he does. You had a nigga that was trying to get somewhere with you. Get to know you and treat you how you want to be treated and you dump him for a nigga that already got a bitch at home."

I could see exactly where this conversation was going. His ego was bruised because I didn't want to fuck with him anymore.

"I didn't dump you because we were never together in the first place. What I did was dumb don't get me wrong but I don't regret the shit. I had to take that chance and see if he and I could be something."

"I can respect that, all I'm saying is you deserve so much more." He told me walking over to my side of the desk.

"Let me guess you want to be the one to give me what I deserve?" I asked him.

I was heartbroken because of what Messiah did to me but whenever I was in Cree's presence it did something to me.

"The only thing I'm trying to give you is this dick." He smirked

"You so nasty" I giggled pushing him away.

"But you like it tho."

"So what if I do, what are you going to do about it?"

"Watch your mouth Juju because I ain't that nigga, I'll put it on you and keep putting it on your ass."

"But seriously I am sorry for the way I handled things. I shouldn't have tried to cut you off all together."

"Don't feel bad ma I understand. But if you do some shit like that again I ain't fucking with your ass anymore." He said. He lifted me out of the chair and sat me on the desk while standing in between his legs. I wrapped my arms around his neck and just stared at him for a minute.

"You want me don't you Juju." He smirked.

"Yea I do." I confessed. "But I can't take it there with you. I need to make sure that you ain't on some hit it and quite it type shit."

"Julani I will tell you this, don't ever let what that fuck nigga did cloud your judgement when it comes to me."

"I hear you, but I'm just letting you know how I feel."

"I can understand that but what I can't understand is how you letting this little thing fuck up like this. I get you loved him but it's not like y'all been together for three years and he was cheating on you. Juju you need to get over it baby, you are too beautiful to be sweating a nigga. If you was with a nigga like me you wouldn't ever have to worry Juju and that's not game that's a promise." He told me

I took a minute to think before I respond to what Cree said. I had to make sure that what I was going to say was the right thing.

"I'm not judging you based off of what he did, I'm just saying I don't want to go through the same thing twice."

"Ight let's say you wait to let me hit it, who's to say that I won't leave after. No period of time will guarantee me staying or going Julani. The only thing you can go by is my word and that's what I'm giving you. Now you can either take my word or be with a nigga or are you going to keep pouting over a nigga that ain't thinking 'bout you."

"You really are trying to be with me like that tho?" I asked needing him to say it just one more time.

"Julani how many times do you want me to say it? I want to fuck with you the long way, while you the long stroke ma."

"Boy get out of here with your annoying ass." I said pushing him away.

"Ain't nothing annoying about me I'm just keeping it a buck. I have to go because I got business to handle but I want you to come see me later."

"I'll think about it." I told him smiling.

"Don't think about it Juju be about it." He said leaning in to kiss me.

I filled up the gap that was between our lips and gave him a quick kiss.

"Come on Julani a nigga can't get more than that?" He chuckled.

"Nah play boy you have to wait until later." I said flirtatiously.

"You got that ma, I'll text you later when I'm done handling my business." He told me.

He went over to the door to open and found Phallyn standing right there looking like she just got caught with her hand in the cookie jar. Jacori was behind her laughing. Cree looked back at me blew me a kiss and then walked out the door.

"You are so nosey." I said to Phallyn getting off of my desk.

"Tell me something I don't know like what happened in here your office door is thick as hell I couldn't hear shit. There's not a trace of sex in the air so I know y'all didn't do the nasty." Phallyn said sitting down

I had to laugh at her because she was really crazy but I loved her though.

"Nothing we talked." I shrugged.

"Bitch don't try me. I know y'all talked I wanna know what y'all talked about."

"He just said that I need to stop pouting over Messiah and get with a real nigga like him."

"You gonna let him hit it ain't you." Phallyn smiled.

"You are such a creep. But I don't know he wants to see me later and the sexual attraction is already there; whatever happens is going to happen." I told her.

"You going to let him hit it and to think you was mad at the fact that I brought him here."

"I don't need you playing match maker and shit."

"Whatever Juju you needed someone to help your stubborn ass. Just say thank you and we can move on."

"Thank you" I said.

You thought you could really make me moan, I had better sex all alone. I had to do your friend now you want me to come back, You must be smoking crack. I'm going elsewhere and that's a fact. Fuck all those nights I moaned out real loud, fuck it, I faked it, I'll rent you out. Fuck all those nights you thought you broke my back well guess what yo, your sex was wack.

Frankee's song fuck you right back started playing from my phone causing Phallyn to start laughing.

"I know you didn't give Messiah that damn ringtone." Phallyn laughed.

"Yea the hell I did."

"You are so fucking petty for that shit. But answer the phone and put that nigga on speaker."

"Hello" I said with an attitude.

"Before you even start going off let me explain." Messiah pleaded

"Put it on speaker." Phallyn mouthed to me.

I pressed the speaker button so Phallyn could hear. "Messiah there is nothing for you to explain because I don't fucking care. I haven't heard from your ass in two months. Two fucking months and now you want to fucking explain!" I shouted.

"Chill with all that yelling and shit."

"Messiah you have no fucking right to tell me what to fucking do. Tell Amara I said I hope she liked how my fucking pussy tasted." I told him and hung up the damn phone. Messiah had a lot of fucking nerve calling my phone talking about he wanted to explain.

"Girl you better than me because I would have hung up as soon as he said let me explain." Phallyn said shaking her head.

"I'm not worried about his ass. I got a new boo or at least I think I do."

"Yassss you better claim that nigga Cree is fine." Phallyn said being ratchet as ever.

"You play entirely too much."

"I'm not playing I'm dead ass serious and when you go see him tonight you better put it on him."

"If I didn't know any better I would think that you were trying to pimp me out." I said looking at her funny.

"I'm not trying to pimp you out I just want you to be happy Juju."

"I know. Enough with all this soft shit though I'm ready to get out of here and go home."

"Ight I'm with you on that one. I'm taking it that you're not coming to the party tonight right."

"Nah." I simply replied.

"Okay well I am shit Jacori's going and I have to make sure no bitch tries to push up on him."

I laughed at her as we headed out of my office. Phallyn was silly as hell but I loved her to death. In the parking lot we said out good byes and went our separate ways. I hoped in my car looking forward to spending the night with Cree. That little conversation that we had in my office really said a lot about his character. I was feeling Cree even though my feelings for Messiah still ran deep. Deep down I still felt like me and Messiah were meant to be together but I had to get over that because he didn't feel the same way.

I pulled into my drive away and decided to let all things Messiah go. As I was walking in my father was leaving out.

"Hey Juju I'm going out to a meeting, I'll see you later I love you."

"I love you too daddy."

"Oh and Messiah is in the house." He said over his shoulder.

The last words made me freeze inside of the door way. What the hell was Messiah doing at my house? I never told my father what happened between us too so he didn't know any better. I quickly got my emotions in check walked in the house and slammed the door behind me. Walking past the living room I saw Messiah sitting on the couch, I completely ignored him and went straight upstairs to my room.

"Julani where are you going!" Messiah yelled after me

I went to slam my bedroom door but he caught it just in time. "Julani stop acting like that and please let me explain.

"Messiah I told you on the phone earlier that there is nothing for you to explain. I no longer care what happened and I don't give a fuck about you." I lied.

"Julani please just listen to me." He pleased with sadness in his eyes.

"Okay." I whispered. I moved away from the door and let him into my room.

I sat on my bed staring at him waiting for him to start explaining.

"After I left you I had every intension of going back to the crib and telling Amara that it was over. Before I could even tell her she broke down crying talking about how she had this feeling that I was going to leave her and if I did leave her she would have no one an all this other shit."

"Wait you mean to tell me that you haven't answered any of my calls or texts because Amara fucking cried."

"I'm all she has Julani. You have a family so I knew you would be good but it's different with her."

"Oh so because she's different she gets to have you." I said with tears starting to form in my eyes.

"It's not like that Juju. For the past nine years I have been that girl's world neither one of us knows what it's like to be without the other and I guess that scares her."

"Messiah get the fuck out of here with that dumb ass excuse I don't want to hear that shit. You sound just as dumb as that excuse that she gave you."

"You just don't understand because your father gave you everything you wanted. You don't know what it's like to be alone. I just can't leave her by her fucking self. I told her that I would always be there for her."

"You wasn't worried about being there for her when you was fucking deep sea diving now did you. You know what fuck you and that bitch; I don't even know why I was jealous of her to begin with." By now the tears were falling freely and I didn't care.

"Julani please don't cry I can't take that shit." He said coming over and wiping my tears.

"Maybe my tears will get you to stay with me for the night." I told him sarcastically.

"Juju don't act like that. I'm not in love with Amara; I'm in love with you. I just need you to give me a little bit longer to figure this shit out."

"You had two months and you need more fucking time."

"Just give me a month and it will be me and you I promise." The look in his eye showed that he was sincere. A part of me wanted to tell him to get out my house and never come back, but the soft side I had for him wasn't having that.

"Fine Messiah you have a month but you better not be fucking that bitch." I told him serious as hell.

"Man I haven't touched that girl since I fucked with you."

"And it better stay that way."

"It will, but Julani I missed you ma." He said kissing me

"Messiah stop it, it ain't even going down like that." I told him trying to push him away.

"I need you Julani stop fighting me" He moaned nibbling on my neck.

The nibbling started at my neck and then went down to my nipples. Once he started sucking on my nipples that was all he wrote. I let him explore my body in more ways than one and I enjoyed them all. As our bodies danced in unison as we did a sexual tango all I could think about was how that bitch no longer had my man.

Chapter Six

I woke up the next morning wrapped in Messiah's arm. I moved them slowly making sure that I didn't wake him up. When I was successful out of the bed I grabbed my phone and went into the bathroom. Messiah and I stayed up all night doing unforgettable things and I never had a chance to call Cree and tell him I wasn't coming. This time around I was going to be a little bit smarter. I wasn't going to cut Cree until I knew for sure that Messiah was serious. Messiah was my heart and there was no denying that, but Cree was the fun type who always kept me smiling.

Looking at my phone I didn't have any missed calls or texts from Cree. I thought it was kind of weird but didn't pay it any mind I hit call button that was by his name and patiently waited for him to answer.

"Wassup Juju" He yawned answering the phone.

"How you know it was me?"

"There is a thing called caller I.D you know"

"Oh yea. Anyway what are you doing you sound like you just woke up."

"I did just wake up. I would have rather woken up to face then a call but it's cool tho."

"My fault about that my father needed me to stay home." I lied effortlessly.

"It's cool ma no need to apologize. I got caught up last night anyway." He told me.

"What were you doing that had you caught up?" I asked

"None of your business."

"Why isn't it any of my business?"

"The less you know the better and you're not my girl so I really don't have to tell you anything." He laughed.

I didn't find a damn thing funny but I wasn't going to let that smart comment get to me. "You're right I'm not your girl so let me get off this phone."

"Julani chill stop acting like that. You know your mine."

"As far as I know I don't belong to anyone but I'm catch up with you later." I told him and hung up the phone.

I turned the water on to wash my face and brush my teeth and then headed out the bathroom. I placed my phone back on the nightstand and cuddled up against Messiah.

"What were you doing in the bathroom?" he asked sleepily.

"I was washing my face and brushing my teeth"

"You must've done a hell of a job because you were in there for a minute." He said turning around to face me.

"You clocking me now?"

"Nah I don't need to clock what's already mine. You know how I get down and I'm sure you value your life so I ain't worried."

He smirked. Messiah had just threatened me and instead of me being upset I was turned on. I was about to respond to his threat when his phone rang. I leaned over to pick it up and Amara's name flashed across the screen.

"Your bitch is calling." I said handing him the phone.

"Don't start no shit." He said before he answered the phone.

I listened as he gave the answers that all nigga's give when they laid up with another bitch. I was tired of him copping a plea so I decided to fuck with him, we went to sleep last night naked which mad everything easier.

I gently pushed him on his back and made my way down south so that I was face to face with my new friend. I opened my mouth up wide and took every inch into my mouth.

"Oh shit….Nothing. Amara chill with all that dumb shit. Yo watch your mouth." Messiah said while trying to hide his moan.

I wrapped my hand around his dick twisting it counter clock wise while my head was moving in a counter clock wise. I picked up the speed and tighten my grip, his dick started to pulsate and I knew he was almost finished.

"Fuck Julani!" Messiah screamed dropping his phone.

I let his dick hit the back of my mouth one last time before his babies shot down my throat. "You might want to pick up that phone now playa." I said getting off the bed.

I left Messiah laid out on the bed with his eyes closed. I walked over to where he dropped his phone and picked it up. Amara's ass was still on the damn phone.

"Messiah, you better not be with that bitch!" I heard her scream when I put the phone to my ear.

"Messiah can't come to the phone right now he 'bout to eat this pussy up." I told her and hung up the phone.

"Julani what the fuck you think you doing?" Messiah asked rising out of the bed.

"Last time you said you were going to tell Amara about us your ass disappeared for two months. All I did was give you an opening to tell."

"I told your ass I was going to tell her this time. You know that shit you did was real foul."

"I don't give a fuck now get the fuck out and don't come back until you tell that bitch wassup." I told him and went into the bathroom.

I don't know what Messiah thought this was but he had the game fucked up. I wasn't going to fall for the same shit twice. He wasn't the only one that could have their cake and eat it too.

*****

After Messiah left I decided to spend time with my father. Between me running Allure I didn't really get to see him as much as

I would've liked. I went over to his room and knocked on the door a couple of times before cracking it open and sticking my head inside.

"Juju I don't know why you're peeking you might as well just come in." My father said never taking his eyes off the TV.

"I wasn't peeking I was just making sure you were up."

"Julani it is damn near two in the afternoon of course I'm up. Come here I wanna talk to you."

I walked in and sat in the chair that was next to my father's bed.

"I saw Messiah leaving not too long ago." He said looking at me.

"Yea he spent the night." I said not trying to tell the whole truth.

"I know he spent the night. My question is where did he spend the night? And don't lie to me Julani"

"Fine daddy he spent the night in my room."

"Julani what the fuck is wrong with you. Don't you k now Messiah has a girl at home. Why are you out here trying to break up happy homes and shit? I raised you better than that and you are too beautiful to be playing second to anyone." My father told me. I know he was upset but whatever was going on between me and Messiah really wasn't any of his business.

"Dad I'm not breaking up anyone's happy home. He is the one that keeps coming to me."

"Then why don't you tell him to leave you alone. I already told you that you need a nigga that is going to be about you and only you. Trust me when I say Messiah ain't that nigga."

"I hear you daddy."

"You saying you hear me but I don't think you do. I'm warning you now fucking with Messiah will leave you hurt."

"Okay daddy." I sighed rolling my eyes.

I didn't want to have this conversation with my father because who I choose to mess with was my business. I wasn't worried about Messiah hurting me because I know he would never do that. Just because he was leaving Amara for me doesn't mean he would do the same thing to me.

"You must be over there thinking about what I said." My father smirked.

"Not really."

"Don't forget that I know you Julani and I know what's best for you and Messiah isn't it."

"Nobody is thinking about Messiah dad. I had enough of this little bonding episode so I'm going to go down to the club and make sure everything is alright for tonight."

"How is the club going?"

"It's fine daddy." I said with a little attitude

"Juju I don't care about you having a fucking attitude get over that shit and quick."

I ignored my father and walked out of his room. My father needed to understand that I was grown and I was going to do whatever I wanted regardless of what he said. I went in my room got dressed and was out the door. I didn't have any intensions of coming back home for a while, shit I was even thinking about getting my own place. Yea getting my own place seemed like it was the right thing to do and it was something that was long overdue anyway.

Chapter Seven

The club was in full effect by the time I decided to leave. I had Phallyn sitting in my office with me but she wasn't trying to leave she wanted to stay.

"Phallyn are you coming or you staying here because I'm more than ready to go."

"You're so annoying. You never want to party." She complained looking down at her phone.

"I don't wanna hear it I had a rough morning and I just want to go to sleep."

"Fine let's go. I can't believe you're rushing me to leave so we can sit in my damn house."

I didn't bother responding I just got up and made my way towards the door. On our way out I stopped at the bar to tell Mikey that I was leaving for the night and too make sure everything was locked up. Mikey was the bartender but I trusted him enough to have keys to the club and close up whenever I didn't feel like staying. As I was walking out the door my phone vibrated, pulling it out my pocket I unlocked the screen and saw a message from Cree that said hurry up. I sent question marks back because I didn't have a clue what he was talking about.

"Jacori and Cree supposed to stop by the club?" I asked Phallyn

"Not that I know of. Why?"

"Cree just sent a text telling me to hurry up."

"Oh. Well I don't know what he and Jacori doing tonight because Jacori ain't answering my calls."

"Why is he screening your calls? Don' tell me you showed him your crazy side already" I asked laughing

"Juju I don't know. Shit I thought everything between us was cool."

"I guess it is cool cause he over there sitting on your car." I told her giggling.

"This nigga got nerve and I don't know why you laughing because Cree is sitting on yours." She pointed out. I turned my head to the left and there he was sitting on the hood of my car. He waved me over with smirk on his face.

"Let me go see what he wants." I said to Phallyn

"Ight if anything just meet me at my house." She said walking off

Walking towards Cree I put something extra in my walk to let him know that I was that bitch. I didn't like how he tried to play me earlier talking about I wasn't his girl then tried to switch it up when he noticed I got an attitude. I couldn't lie though he was looking like my future baby daddy as he sat on the hood of my car. He had on a pair of sweats with a black hoodie and a pair of wheat Tims. He had his snap back towards the back sitting low with a simple gold chain hanging from his neck. Just the sight of him had me ready to throw my panties to the wind, but I had to pull myself together because he wasn't getting any of this."

"Ma why you taking your sweet ass time walking over here like I'm not waiting for you?" Cree asked.

"Why are you sitting on my car Cree?"

"Damn I can't get a hello, I just get straight attitude." He said carefully getting off my car.

"Hi Cree." I said and got in my car.

"Julani I don't know what your problem is but you need to lose that attitude. I'm not that bitch nigga ight, your little mean ass is going to show me some respect."

I sat and watched as Cree got in the car and couldn't believe how he was talking to me. I loved a nigga that could take charge but I wasn't going to let him punk me like that.

"The only bitch nigga I see is the one sitting next to me." I smirked. The smirk didn't last long because Cree yanked my face towards him and squeezed the shit out of my cheeks.

"Watch your mouth Julani." He said and mushed me

"Don't put your hands on me I don't play that shit."

"Yea whatever. You coming home with me tonight."

He reached over plugged his address into the GPS and reclined his seat. Cree had a lot of nerve and was cocky as shit but I was feeling it. I pulled off following the directions that the GPS gave me. During the drive I would look over at Cree and just wonder what it was that he was thinking about. I wanted to ask but every time I asked Cree something he told me it wasn't any of my business. I wanted to know more about him because he really was intriguing. It just seemed like I would never really get to know him.

*****

"Don't be scared now, you wanted to get to know me right well it all starts with you coming inside." Cree said holding his front door open for me.

I slowly walked in and stood by his front door because I didn't know where else to go.

"Let me show you my house." He said taking my hand in his.

His townhouse was really beautiful he had the walls painted a light grey color which was something that I have never seen before. He had black leather furniture in the living room with all black steel appliances in the kitchen. When we got to his bedroom I was in awe; he had a fire place in his bedroom with a California king sleigh bed right across from it. The color scheme in his room was black and gold. All the dressers were black with accents of gold on them; I didn't know what Cree did for a living but whatever it was he was making good money from it.

"Your house is beautiful; I know the ladies must love this fire place." I said.

"You would think that right." He chuckled.

"Why are you laughing?" I asked not getting the joke.

"You must really think I'm the player type."

"I only know what you tell me and that's a lot."

"Well let me tell you this I have never brought a female to my house so consider yourself lucky." He said taking off his hoodie. I watched him as he took off his clothes until he was a wife beater and his briefs. Cree's body was amazing, he was built but not overly built he had just enough muscles. His right arm was covered in tattoos that I just wanted to touch and trace over the lines.

"You might want to close your mouth before you drool all over my floor." Cree laughed.

"Oh shut up and I find it hard to believe that you don't bring females here."

"I don't honestly." He shrugged and got on his bed. "You gonna come lay down with me or you wanna continue to stand in the middle of my floor?"

"Do you have a shirt I could put on?"

"Yea check that middle draw over there."

I walked over to his dresser and looked through his shirts. I found one that was a Brooklyn net's shirt and pulled it out the draw.

"Do you mind if I change in your bathroom?" I asked him

"I would rather you change in front of me but you know if you feel uncomfortable you can change in the bathroom."

I felt like he was challenging me and me being who I am I never back down from a challenge. I kicked off my sneakers and pulled down my seven jeans while I looked him in his eyes. I slowly peeled off my shirt letting him get a good enough peek before I through on his t-shirt.

"Don't try to tease me Juju if you want me come and get me."

"Cree nobody wants your ass." I laughed as I got in bed.

"Trust me a lot of people want me but I only want one person and why you all the way over there I told you before I won't bite you unless you ask."

I moved a little closer to Cree but I kept enough space between us so we weren't touching each other. "Cree why do you like to play games." I asked randomly.

"What games do I play?"

"If you want to be with me why don't you just come out and say it."

"What's understood shouldn't have to be explained."

"It's not that simple though. If you want to be with me then I'm going to need you to say it because actions don't always speak louder than words. Sometimes words can give you something that actions can't."

"You're right about words giving you something that actions can't because your actions and words don't match Juju. When we talk a deaf person can hear that we are into each other the chemistry is that real but your actions say something total different."

"What do you mean my actions say something different?"

"Julani don't play dumb because you too smart for that ma. Your actions show that you would rather fuck with that nigga Messiah than to get with a real nigga. I may not like it but I do respect your choice ma."

"I wouldn't rather fuck with anyone. Neither one of y'all are claiming me as yours so I'm doing what every nigga does and keeping my options open."

"Your telling me if I made shit official you would leave that nigga alone?"

"Only one way to find out." I smirked.

"Come get on top."

I shrugged my shoulders and straddled him with my arms crossed over my chest. He put his hands on my hips as he gazed into my eyes. I shifted the way I was sitting because his dick started to grow and he was making it jump.

"Julani I'm a keep it real with you. I want you in more ways than one. I want you to be my ridah, my relief from all the stress. I want you to be the calm before the storm."

"You talk a good game you know that." I said trying to hide the fact that I was blushing.

"This isn't a game this is real shit. Julani you are beautiful, smart and independent. Your mouth is smart as hell but I like that feisty shit. I'm trying to lock you down and throw away the key but you be playing with a nigga. You too caught up in a high school crush. You stuck on stupid for a boy that keeps benching your ass for his star player when you could be with a nigga that's trying to make you the MVP on his team."

"I hear everything you saying Cree." I told him. I climbed off of him laid my head on his chest and wrapped my leg around him.

"You saying you hear me but you're not saying that you're with me though. Are you with me Julani? I promise you that if you are I will give you the moon and the stars."

I didn't want to answer him right away because I wasn't sure I could give him what he wanted. A part of me wanted to be with Cree but the other side was still caught up in Messiah. I had given Messiah a month to tell Amara what was up between us. Within that month I was going to see what was up with Cree but I was still going to see Messiah. I was so close to having Messiah to myself that I couldn't just throw things away for Cree. But at the same time Cree was saying all of the right things.

"I'm with you." I whispered. I figured I could just fuck with Cree until things with Messiah got better.

"If you with me then you're only with me Julani. If I find out that you still fucking with that nigga I promise you that you will be buried six feet under right next to his ass."

"Is that a threat?" I asked

"It's whatever you want it to be but you heard what the fuck I said. I don't play that side nigga shit." He said and kissed me on the forehead.

"I forgot to text Phallyn and tell her that I'm staying over here." I said and got out the bed. I went into my bag and grabbed my phone but instead of texting Phallyn I sent Messiah a text telling him that I missed him and wanted to see him tomorrow. I was about to put my phone down when a text came through. I smiled at the sight of Messiah's name.

Messiah

Bitch don't text my man's phone, he doesn't want your dumb ass. All he wanted to do was get his dick wet and now that you served your purpose you can crawl back into the fucking hole you came out from.

I had to read the text two more times to make sure that I was reading it right. I couldn't believe that Amara had the nerve to text me some shit like that. I guess that little fight we had didn't teach her a lesson. I sent a text back telling her that she could have Messiah for now because I would have him in the end. I made sure that the text was sent before I climbed back into bed with Cree.

"You ight?" He asked sensing that I had an attitude.

"Yea it was just my father. We had got into an argument earlier and I forgot all about it until I looked at my phone."

"Let me ease your mind" Cree said placing his body on top of mines.

"Cree what are you doing?"

"Shhhh" he whispered

He lifted my shirt over my head exposing my hard nipples. He started rolling my nipples in between his fingers causing me to tension up a little from the sensation.

"I don't think we should be doing this." I told him.

"Why your old nigga going to get mad?" Cree asked looking me in the eyes.

I ignored what he said and slipped out of my panties. I took his hand and moved it so he could feel my wetness. "I'm not worried about anyone besides you." I told him before kissing him.

Everything after that was just intense and on a whole other level. We explored every part of each other's body. It felt like we were making love and that we were one. The feeling I got from the sex we had scared me a little because I had never connected with someone like that. I thought sex with Messiah was amazing, sex with Cree was indescribable. There were no words that could explain the passion that we shared; it was just one of those things that you had to experience in order to understand.

Chapter Eight

"I don't care what the fuck you have to do just handle that shit by the time I get there." I heard Cree yell into the phone.

I looked over at the clock that was on his nightstand to see what time it was. It was one in the afternoon and Cree was yelling like my ass wasn't trying to sleep. I sat up in bed and rubbed the sleep out of my eyes. I listen as Cree kept going on and on about how if he had to handle shit his self then a lot of people would be sorry.

"My fault Juju did I wake you up?"

"Kind of. What was all of that about?" I asked him

"Nothing just business. What are you doing for the day?"

"I don't have any plans I was going to go over to Phallyn's house and then hit the club later." I told him.

"Ight I may swing by the club later tonight and check on you, but I got to handle something right now, so get dressed so I can drop you off at your car."

"Damn you kicking me out already, you could have at least taken me out to breakfast." I giggled while getting out of bed

"Juju you know it ain't even like that, I just have something I have to do."

"I'm only playing with you. Could you get me a wash cloth and tooth brush please."

"They're in the closet right next to the bathroom. You need to learn your way around if you gonna be staying here."

"Who said I was moving in with you? Don't you think that's moving too fast?"

"It might be moving too fast for you but it's not for me. I already told you that I want you the rest is up to you Julani."

"I hear you talking player."

I left the room before Cree could say anything else. It was cute that he wanted me to move in with him but I wasn't ready for all of that. I looked in the closet grabbed a wash rag and a tooth brush and went into the bathroom. I looked at my reflection in the mirror and my hair was all over the place. I finger combed my curls and tried to make my hair as presentable as I could.

"Juju hurry up!" I heard Cree yell

I quickly washed my face and brushed my teeth before I went back into the bedroom. I grabbed my bag and followed him out the house and into his car. The whole car ride was awkward because Cree was on the phone going off on someone. I sat on my phone trying not to ease drop but I couldn't help it. Whoever Cree was going off on was lucky that they weren't in Cree's presence.

"My bad bout that shit but nigga's act like money's not the motive." Cree said hanging up the phone and pulling into the clubs parking lot.

"And just how do you get your money?" I asked

"That's another conversation for a different day."

"Yea I bet it is. How can you want to be with me but you keep so many secrets?"

"I'm not keeping secrets I don't feel like it's the right time for me to put you on."

"You can't put me on but you want me to move in with you." I smirked

"Those are too different areas Juju; you can't get hurt by moving in with me. If I tell you what I do you could get hurt."

"It doesn't even matter because I already know. You do the same shit Messiah and my father does."

"How do you know that?" he asked with a raised eye brow

"Phallyn told me because unlike you Jacori doesn't keep secrets from her."

"It was never a secret I just felt that you didn't need to know. You keeping the fact that you already know what I do from me is a secret. But it's cool I'm not going to hold that against you. Never compare Jacori and Phallyn's relationship to ours ight?"

"Ok but you couldn't hold that against me even if you tired. But let me get going I need a shower and I wanna change out these clothes." I said unbuckling my seat belt.

"Ight I'ma call you later. Give me a kiss."

I leaned over to kiss him and let my lips linger there for a while.

"Be good ight ma." Cree said pulling away from me.

"I'm always good." I smiled getting out the car.

"Yea ight stay that way and remember what I said about that fuck nigga."

"I told you I was with you Cree so I'm with you." I told him winking and going over to my car.

I pulled off headed towards Phallyn's house so she could help me figure this shit out. I was feeling like a hoe the way that I slept with Messiah and Cree. I wanted Messiah but I didn't know if I could last a month waiting for him. I was so confused between the both of them and even though I had Cree I was still jealous of the fact that Amara would be with Messiah for another month.

*****

I pulled up to Phallyn's condo ready to vent and find a solution to all my problems. As I was getting out the car I saw Jacori coming out of the building. He was fine I guess that's why he and Cree ran together. The cute ones always ran in packs.

"Wassup Juju, you going to see your girl?" He asked helping me out the car.

"Yea, I just left Cree's crib but he had some business to handle." I told him

"Oh shit he took you to the crib; he must really be feeling you." Jacori said sounding surprised.

"He said he is but I don't know." I shrugged.

"I have known Cree since we were young, and everything he says he means. Now I'm not telling you that you should be with him I'm just saying he is a real thorough bread."

"I hear you Jacori and for right now we just seeing how things play out."

"Ight Juju." Jacori said and walked away.

I headed into the building and went straight for Phallyn's apartment; I was going to knock on her door when I noticed that it was open.

"Phallyn why is your front door open? Girl someone going to kidnap you." I said walking in.

"What are you yelling for and no one is going to kidnap me; if they do they won't keep me for long especially with my attitude." Phallyn said coming out her bathroom.

"You're right about that." I laughed sitting on her couch.

"Where were you last night because I waited up to get a text from you but I never got one?"

"Cree took me to his house, made us official then put it on me in the worse way."

"You're such a hoe." Phallyn giggled.

"Bitch don't call me a hoe." I said throwing a pillow at her.

"Don't get mad at me I'm just calling it how I see it. You slept with Cree not even 24 hours after you had sex with Messiah."

"I know it was wrong but lawd sex with Cree felt so right."

"You really need to figure this shit out because you starting to look sloppy in these streets and that's me telling you that as a friend."

"I respect it but I can't leave Messiah alone."

"He acted like you didn't exist for two months and now that he's back you can't leave him alone. On top of that he has a bitch and I'm letting you know now this whole jealous thing that you got going on you need to get over it and fast."

"You just don't understand." I told her shaking my head.

"Maybe you're right, I don't understand but what I do understand is that fucking with Messiah isn't going to do anything but hurt you. From what I can see Cree really likes your stubborn ass and you would be a fool not to give him a chance." Phallyn said giving it to me straight.

"I hear you I really do but how am I just going to let that bitch Amara win. She doesn't deserve him she doesn't even know what to do with that."

"Let me guess you know what to do with that?" Phallyn smirked

"Of course I do which is why he keeps coming back." I said sounding like a true bird.

"Julani do you know how dumb you sound right now but you know what I'ma let you learn for yourself."

"Ok enough with this conversation because I see that attitudes are coming in to play. What you cooking I'm starving." I said

"I'm not cooking your hoe ass shit." Phallyn laughed getting up and going in the kitchen.

"Yea whatever I'm going to wash my ass and change clothes because we going to the club later on."

"I'm not going anywhere Jacori is supposed to come back over here later."

"Oh shit Jacori must be the one because your ass stays trying to go to the club."

"I like him I really do." Phallyn blushed

"I'm happy for you Phallyn." I said honestly

"Thanks if you would just give Cree a chance I could be happy for you too." She replied sarcastically.

"Don't worry about me ok. Just worry about having my food ready by the time I get out the shower."

"I'm not your fucking maid. Cook for yourself." Phallyn laughed.

"But you love me." I told her and walked towards her room.

I went through the bag of clothes that I had and found a cute little black dress that had the sides cut out to wear. I wasn't in the mood to wear heels so I pulled out my gladiator sandals. I laid the outfit out on the bed just to make sure that everything looked right. I added a couple gold bangles and a gold watch and was pleased with my outfit. I grabbed a towel and a wash cloth and jumped in the shower so I could wash the previous 24 hours off of me.

Chapter Nine

"You lucky I love your ass. I'm not trying to hear Jacori's mouth because I'm going out tonight." Phallyn complained.

"Shut up Jacori ain't going to care I already sent Cree a text telling them both of us was going to Allure and it's not like you going to shake your ass you going to help me take care of business."

"As much as I help you take care of business I should open my own club or own half of yours." Phallyn joked.

"When do you graduate?" I asked her

"Not for another year but that doesn't even matter because I already know everything I need to know I'm just waiting for that degree."

"You right you do help me a lot so I feel it's only right that I make you part owner of the club and when you're ready to open that business I got you." I told her smiling.

"Juju don't play like that are you serious?" she excitedly asked.

"Yea I'm serious you have been my backbone our whole friendship and now it's time for me to be yours."

"Julani you have always been my backbone girl you already know I got you for any and everything."

"I know and that's why I love your annoying ass but tomorrow I will have the papers drawn up so you can sign them and then everything will be legit."

"Ayeee. Let's go celebrate." Phallyn said dancing in her seat.

"Your ass was just complaining about going to the club and now you wanna go shake your ass." I laughed.

"Yesss" she sang. "Now I have a reason to go to the club bitch this is big you know we have to turn up now."

I shook my head at Phallyn because her ass was too silly. The rest of the ride to the club we talked about ideas that we both had for the club. When we pulled up to Allure the parking lot was packed and the line was around the corner. We got out and as we were walking in I noticed Amara in the line.

"Juju watch out." Phallyn said. I turned just in time to avoid the pole that was in front of the club.

"What the hell was you looking at that were so important?" Phallyn asked as we walked inside.

"Amara's ass was outside on the line with a group of females." I said a little annoyed.

"Julani don't let her get to you especially at your place of business. Fuck that bitch she's'bout to pay money to get into your club so pay her ass no mind." Phallyn said.

"You mean our club but you right, I'm not going to be petty tonight. I'm going to keep it calm, cool, and collected." I told her. I didn't have any plans of getting out of character tonight but if Amara tried anything I was going to shut shit down.

"I hope so Juju. I'm 'bout to go to the bar I'll meet you in your office."

I left Phallyn at the bar and continued to my office. I pushed in the code and opened the door to see Messiah sitting my chair looking out to the dance floor.

"Messiah what are you doing here? Better yet what are you doing in my office?" I asked

"I was waiting for you." He answered. He got up and walked over to me with lust filled eyes. I didn't know what Messiah thought was about to happen but it wasn't going to go down like that in my office.

"Waiting for me for what?" I asked dodging his hug and taking a seat in my chair.

"You can't hug me now? I thought we were in a good place?" he questioned.

"We will not be in a good place until you tell Amara what's up and from the text that I got last night she still doesn't know."

"You gave me a month remember." He had the nerve to say.

"I know I gave you a month but if you were really about me then you would have told her ass the same day that you left my house. You wouldn't have gotten mad at me for talking to her on the phone. You ain't shit but a fucking liar!" I yelled.

"Julani what do you want me to do huh? I am all Amara has, we have been together since we were 18. Do you know how hard it is to just leave someone that you have all that history with?"

"Do you know how it feels to watch the man you love be with another chick?" I cried.

"Julani don't do that." Messiah said leaning over the desk and wiping my tears.

"Don't touch me." I told him pushing his hand away. "Messiah my feelings for you are real but I'm not going to play second to anyone. It's either going to be all about me or all about her."

"Julani I would never ask you to play second and I have way to much respect for you to even think that you would be a side chick."

"So what are you saying?" I asked confused.

"I'm saying that I just need a month. Just give me a month to fix shit okay." He pleaded.

"I already told you I will give you a month but we won't be fucking until you told her."

"Come on Juju you can't do that to me"

"Yes the hell I can now get out my office and go get your bitch."

"I'm talking to my bitch right now." He smirked.

"I'm not your bitch I'm THE BITCH. But I'm talking about your other bitch, she outside standing in line." I laughed.

"Why you lying?" he asked and looked out my glass window.

"No I'm not. Look at that she's over there talking to Phallyn how about we go over there and say hello."

"The fuck she doing here?" Messiah mumbled. "I'm 'bout to go take her ass home don't go down there starting no shit."

"I'm not going to start anything." I smiled.

We left my office and made our way through the crowd and over to the bar where Phallyn and Amara was. Walking up to them I could see that they were having an intense conversation. The club was too loud so I couldn't hear anything.

"Ahem. Is everything okay over here?" I politely asked.

"Everything is cool I was having a drink when Amara and her two body guards walked up to me questioning me like they the feds." Phallyn said sipping her drink.

"Amara what are you doing here?" Messiah asked her

"Messiah this has nothing to do with you." Amara said.

"Amara if you want to ask questions about me then ask me don't question my best friend." I said making sure I didn't lose my temper.

"Then let me ask you this, why is your hoe ass fucking my man?!" Amara yelled.

"Amara let's fucking go we're not 'bout to do this shit here." Messiah said yoking Amara up.

"Messiah you better get your hands off of her." One of Amara's manly friends said.

"Bitch no one is worried about you." Messiah said

"Bitch! I'll show you your bitch." The girl said getting ready to swing at Messiah.

I looked over at the bouncer and signaled for him to come over. The girl was taking a step forward ready to swing at Messiah when I stuck my foot out and tripped her.

"I'ma need y'all to get out of my club with all this ratcheness." I said laughing at the girl trying to get off the floor.

"Bitch did you just trip my sister." The other girl said.

"Uh huh sweetie, you don't wanna fuck with that one because I will do more than trip your ass." Phallyn said getting in the girls face.

"Do we have a problem here?" Steve asked.

"No but I would appreciate it if you would escort these ladies out of my club."

"No problem Julani."

Phallyn and I watched as Messiah damn near dragged Amara out the club and Steve pushing her two friends out.

"You know you're wrong for tripping that girl right?" Phallyn laughed.

"I wasn't going to let her manly ass hit Messiah."

"I don't know why you so worried about him" Phallyn said rolling her eyes. "Where did he come from anyway?"

"He was in the office waiting for me." I answered shaking my head.

"Y'all two are something else."

"I didn't tell him to come here he came on his own."

"Yea whatever." Phallyn said looking down at her phone.

"Who you texting that got you smiling?"

"Jacori he said him and Cree are outside and they want us to come out."

Before we went to the parking lot we ran to the bathroom to make sure that our appearance was up to par. After fingering my curls and Phallyn putting extra lip gloss we made our way outside. When we got out to the parking lot there were a crowd of people forming a circle.

"What's going on?" Phallyn asked one of the girls that was standing on the outside of the circle.

"I don't know two fine ass men are talking about some bitch. But the crazy thing is one of them got a tight grip on some chick while telling the other nigga to stay away from his bitch."

At that point I already knew who the two men she was referring to were. I pushed my way through the circle to see Messiah and Cree staring each other down.

"What the fuck is going on?" I asked getting both of their attention.

"This nigga trying to tell me to stay away from his chick." Cree smirked at me.

"Julani tell this nigga that you want to be with me." Messiah said.

"Messiah don't fucking act like I'm not here." Amara said yanking away from Messiah.

"Amara I don't give a fuck if you here or not. Now Julani tell this nigga that you're mine."

"Julani you want this fuck nigga?" Cree asked.

I didn't know what to do here I was at my damn place of business and these nigga's were trying to make me choose. I looked over at Phallyn for support but she just shrugged her shoulders.

"Messiah you already know what the deal is."

"Amara I don't want you to be with you, I wish I could have told you this at a different time but shit ain't no time like the present." Messiah shrugged. Everyone in the crowd gasped including me.

"Messiah you going to leave me for this bitch, this bitch can't love you like I can!" Amara screamed.

Jealous: The Bitch That Has My Man

"Amara calm down I said what I had to say." Messiah said.

After that it was like everything went in slow motion I ran over to Messiah jumped in his arms and kissed the shit out of him. Before the kiss could even end Amara grabbed me by my hair and pulled me to the ground. Her friends tried to jump in but Phallyn jumped on both of their asses. Amara was getting the best of me until Messiah grabbed her off of me and Cree grabbed me.

"Amara get the fuck out of here I said what I had to say" Messiah said giving her the death stare.

"Messiah you a bitch nigga and don't worry what goes around comes around Julani!" she screamed before walking away.

"You made your bed and now you have to live with it. I hope you happy being the side chick." Cree whispered in my ear before walking away.

By now all the bouncers came out side and cleared out the parking lot. I looked over at Phallyn to say thank you for having my back but she just shook her head and followed Jacori to his car. I stood in the middle of the parking lot embarrassed that I had just got my ass beat but it was worth it because I finally got my nigga.

Chapter Ten

"Julani your phone keep vibrating and shit. It better not be that nigga blowing up your phone." I heard Messiah say.

Ignored him and rolled over and tried falling back to sleep. My phone had been ringing off the hook ever since last night.

"Julani you better answer that phone before I break that shit." Messiah said getting out of bed.

I sat up and thought about saying something smart but decided against. I reached over to the nightstand grabbed my phone and answered it without looking at the caller ID.

"Hello." I answered sounding every bit of annoyed.

"Julani I don't know where your hot ass is but you better get your ass to this house now." My father demanded.

"Daddy what's wrong?" I asked a little concerned.

"Everything will be fine as long as you bring your ass home now and bring Messiah with you too." He said and hung up the phone.

I looked at my phone confused as hell my father has never hung up the phone on me. I didn't know what his problem was but I didn't appreciate him talking to me like I was still a child.

"Who was that on the phone?" Messiah asked coming back into the room with a bowl of cereal.

"My father he wants to talk to the both of us."

"About what?" He asked. He got on the bed eating the bowl of cereal while I watched him. "Why you looking at me like that."

"How you come in here with only one bowl of cereal?" I wasn't a big cereal eater but he could have brought me some fruit or something.

"You don't even like cereal like that, so what you mad for."

"I'm mad because you didn't even think to bring me something to eat."

"Julani you can't seriously have an attitude over this small shit." Messiah said putting his bowl down.

"Messiah just forget it you don't understand" I told him. I was mad but at the same time I was over the whole thing.

"Then help me to understand Julani." Messiah said looking me deep in my eyes.

"You can stop giving me that look because that's not helping the situation. Now let's go before my father calls me again." I pushed him out of my face and then got out of bed.

"What does he want anyway?" Messiah asked finishing up his cereal.

"I don't know but he seemed pissed off so you need to hurry up."

I went into the bathroom to take a quick shower so that I could hurry and get to my father's house I hoped like hell that no one told him about last night. After everything that happened in the parking lot. Messiah and I got in our cars and I followed him to a condo that he kept for when he wanted to get away from Amara. As soon as we got inside we couldn't keep our hands off of each other. We had sex in every room in this house; just thinking about it had me feeling hot and bothered.

I took the showerhead down and made sure the water was warm before placing it in between my legs. I lead back on the wall as the pressure from the water hit my clit with intensity. I turned the nozzle on the shower head so there was a little bit pressure.

"Mhmmm" I moaned softly. Images of what happened last night between me and Messiah started to flash in my mind.

I was so caught up in what I had going on that I never heard Messiah come in the bathroom. By the time I realized it he was already in the shower whispering in my ear.

"If you wanted to be pleasured all you had to do was let me know Juju."

He took the shower head out of my hand and placed it back above us. He took my hands and placed them on the wall that was in front of me causing the water to fall on my head. He grabbed a handful of my hair and yanked my head back. With his other hand he started to fondle my breasts paying extra attention to my nipples.

"Tell me you love me Juju." Messiah said continuing to play with my nipples

"I love you" I moaned

"Arch it." He said slapping my ass.

I arched my back and poked my butt out as far as I could. Messiah still had a grip on my hair as he placed his dick at my open. Every time he would push the head in and I would back my ass up to get him to go deeper he would pull out. I was tired of him playing with my anxious ass. Between what I did with the shower head and him pulling my hair I was more than ready for some dick.

"Messiah stop playing and give it to mhmmmm." I moaned.

I couldn't even get the last word out because Messiah slipped into my honey pot and went as deep as possible. He let go of my hair and grabbed onto my hips as he pumped in and out of me. The water was going down my body making the sound of his pelvis hitting my ass louder.

"Ahhhh Messiah." I screamed.

Messiah was making sure that I was feeling everything that he had to offer. I swore I was in ecstasy. Everything felt so right that I was cumming within minutes.

"Slow down" I told Messiah so that I could catch my breath.

"Take this dick and shut up." He said.

I leaned up with my back still arched and placed my heads on my head. Messiah cupped my breasts and started biting my neck. I was sure that I was going to have a couple of passion marks on my neck because Messiah wasn't playing. He was fucking the shit out of me and I was loving every minute of it. I came two more times before I was tired and had enough. I leaned back on the wall so that I had support and started throwing it back meeting him at every thrust.

"Let me taste you cum papi." I moaned as Messiah dug deeper.

"You wanna taste daddy's cum." Messiah grunted.

I nodded my head yes because I couldn't get any words to form.

"Then come taste it" Messiah said sliding out of me.

I quickly turned around and got on my knees and put the tip of Messiah's dick in my mouth. His cum slide down my throat causing me to gag, swallowing cum wasn't something that I normally did but for Messiah I would.

"Let me find out you're a freak behind closed doors." Messiah said helping me up.

"Well now that we can finally be together I can show you what a real bitch does to keep her man." I smirked.

"Julani don't do that." Messiah sighed.

"I'm not doing anything I'm just saying that I'm going to get the ring and the baby that Amara never had."

"Oh you wanna have my baby and my last name?" He asked hugging me from the back.

"I don't know maybe it depends on how you act but let's hurry up and get to my father's house." I told him.

We quickly washed each other up, got dressed and hopped in the car to go to my house. While in my car I checked my phone and I have five missed calls, two of them were from Phallyn and the other three were from my father. I already knew I was going to hear a mouthful from him so I prepared myself a head of time to hear a lecture about whatever I did that was wrong.

*****

Messiah and I walked into the house that I shared with my father and it was quiet, a little too quiet for my liking. We walked into the living room to see if my father was there but he wasn't.

"Daddy!" I yelled sitting on the couch.

"Why you yelling instead of just going to find him like a normal person?" Messiah asked mushing me in the head

"I don't feel like getting up plus he called me over here I shouldn't have to find him."

"Julani the fuck are you yelling for. This is a house not the fucking outdoors." My father said walking into the living room mean mugging us.

"Ok. Why do you seem so upset?" I asked

"Messiah." My father said hitting him with a nod. My father and Messiah were close which is why I didn't understand why my father gave him one of those nods that you give someone when you don't really fuck with them.

"Daddy what's the matter?" I asked again hoping to get an answer this time around.

"Julani what happened at Allure last night?" When he asked that all the color drained from my skin. I got nervous as hell because I knew that someone had called and told him what happened.

"Nothing happened." I lied just to see how much he knew.

"Julani don't fucking lie to me. Now what the fuck happened?"

"Nothing I got into a little fight. It wasn't anything worth someone calling you for. I'm grown anyway so I don't see why people have to call you about my business."

"They call me because you are my business and from what I heard it wasn't a little fight." My father said.

"It wasn't anything serious." I shrugged.

"You getting your ass beat for that nigga over there is something serious."

My father turned from me to Messiah and I instantly froze. The look on both of their faces showed no emotion and that scared the shit out of me. Messiah wasn't pussy but at the same time my father wasn't anything to play with.

"Messiah I expected more from you especially since I consider you my son. I've been rocking with you since you were 18. I was the one that put you on that gave you a chance and this is how you repay me by having my daughter fighting in these streets over your ass. You didn't even step to me like a real nigga and let me know that you were feeling my daughter I had to hear it from the grape vine. I'ma tell you this shit though and I'm only going to tell you it once. I put this on my dead wife if you hurt Julani in any type of way and I do mean in any type of way I promise you that I will set you up with the firing squad." My father threatened.

"King it won't even have to come to that but you should already know I don't take kindly to threats. I understand Julani is your daughter and you want the best for her so I'ma let that rock. Julani I'll catch up with you later." Messiah said. He got up kissed me on the forehead and walked towards the door. I watched him walk away and it took everything in me not jump up and leave with him. I knew if I would have done that then it would've only made shit worse

"Daddy why did you have to go and do that? You already know Messiah wouldn't do anything to hurt me." I pouted

"Julani what don't you get, he just up and left Amara who he been with for damn near nine years. What makes you think that he won't do the same shit to you?"

"I don't care that he left Amara there wasn't nothing really between them anyway."

"Yea ight Julani if you think he's really going to leave Amara alone then you got another thing coming. Just be smart ight." My father said.

He got up kissed me on the cheek and left the living room. I sat there caught up in my thoughts. I couldn't believe that Messiah had stood up to my father, but it did make me respect him a little bit more. If Messiah could stick up to my father for our relationship then so could I. I didn't care what anyone thought or how anyone felt. Messiah was mine and I wasn't going to let go of that no time soon for anyone.

Chapter Eleven

I was at my lawyer's office picking up the contract for Phallyn. Phallyn has been there for me through thick and thin and I wanted her to be part owner of Allure with me.

"Thank you Marty." I said shaking his hand.

"No problem Julani if you need anything else let me know." He smiled.

I nodded my head letting him know that I would call him if there was anything else. I left his office and went to go sit in my car. I hadn't heard from Phallyn since the whole thing with Amara went down at Allure and that was damn near two weeks ago. I had been calling her but she just straight ignored every phone call. I wasn't going to lie I was hurt because I didn't understand what reason she had to ignore my calls. Even though she was ignoring me I still went ahead and had the contracts drawn up so that she would be part owner of Allure because at the end of the day she was still my best friend and this is something I wanted for her.

I picked up my phone and decided to call her again. The phone rang five times and I was about to hang up when Phallyn answered the phone.

"Hello?" Phallyn answered dryly.

"Phallyn where the hell you been? I know that you seen all my missed calls."

"Yea I saw them." She responded.

I removed the phone from my ear to make sure that I had dialed the right number. "Phallyn what's up with the attitude?' I question starting to catch an attitude of my own.

"Nothing Julani." She sighed.

"Stop lying and tell me what's up."

"I don't feel like talking about this over the phone."

"Then I'm coming to your house." I said hanging up the phone.

I wasn't sure what exactly Phallyn's problem was but we were going to figure it out. Phallyn and I had been friends for too long to just throw it away over some bullshit. I drove to her house trying to come up with different reasons why she would be mad but I couldn't come up with any. I shrugged it off and figured that I would find out soon enough when I got to her house. It didn't take long for me to get there but when I did I got nervous. I parked my car got out and walked up to the door. I knocked a couple of times before Phallyn swung the door open and moved out the way for me to walk in. She slammed the door behind me, walked right passed me and flopped on the couch.

"Well hello to you too." I said sarcastically. I sat down across from her and looked at her as she stared at me with a blank expression.

"Julani what did you come over here for? I told you I didn't want to talk 'bout this over the phone, I never told you're ass to come over."

"I never needed an invite before so why do I need one now."

"I'm not saying that you need one no…"

"We not going to keep going back and forth with these slick ass comments. Just keep it a buck and tell me what the hell the problem is. We are both grown and we should be able to talk this shit out." I said cutting her off.

"What happened that night was fucking embarrassing for both you and me. How you out there fighting over a nigga that you took from someone else and then get your ass beat by the bitch you took the nigga from. On top of that you out here playing with people's feelings and shit like everything is a game. I don't know what happened to you but you're not acting like the Julani I know. I knew your crush on Messiah was serious but I thought that you would get over it after a while but I guess I was wrong. All I'ma say is this you need to watch Messiah because he doesn't love you he loves the thought of you!"

"Why can't people just let me live?" I ask frustrated. "Look I know what happened in that parking lot was wrong but I didn't start that. I didn't ask Messiah to make that announcement he did that on his own. Do I feel bad about taking Messiah from Amara? No, I don't because she don't deserve him all she does is spend his money. As far as people getting hurt the only person that got hurt was Cree and I never meant for that to happen."

"Did you even have feelings for Cree or was he just something to do?" Phallyn asked.

"I did have feelings for Cree and I was willing to give him a chance. But when Messiah declared his love for me in front of everyone how could I turn that down when that is all I ever wanted. I know I owe Cree an apology and I plan on giving him one I just haven't run into him yet."

"Well you can give it to him when he gets here." Phallyn smirked.

"Why is he coming over here?" I asked

"Him and Jacori coming over to chill, by the time you called I had already told them to come over." She shrugged.

"Oh okay. Are we cool now though?"

"Yea we cool. You know I love you Julani regardless of the dumb things that you may do. I just couldn't talk to you after everything that happened because I was ready to beat your ass."

"You would've tried to beat my ass but I would have fucked you up." I laughed.

"Like you fucked Amara up." Phallyn laughed.

"Shut up she got lucky but here these are for you." I told her handing her a folder.

"What is this?" She started skimming the papers and a smile spread across her face. "Oh my god Julani you really want me to be your business partner."

"Of course you're my best friend." I smiled.

"Thank you!" she cheered.

We got up gave each other a hug but it was cut short because there was a knock at the door. Phallyn was too busy looking at the contract so I got up to answer the door. I didn't bother looking through the peep hole I just opened the door.

"Wassup Julani, where Phallyn at?" Jacori asked giving me a hug.

"She's in the living room." I told him but never taking my eyes off of Cree.

Jacori walked past me and left Cree and I standing at the door way. I wanted to say something but no words would form.

"Wassup Julani." Cree said pushing past me.

I quickly closed the front door and grabbed his arm before he got too far. "Cree wait." He turned around and looked at me but didn't say anything.

"Can I talk to you?" I asked him.

"Yea wassup?"

"Do you mind if we go outside?" I asked leading the way out the door.

We sat on the steps that lead up to Phallyn's house, for a couple of minutes we just stared at each other. I didn't know what he was thinking about but I knew I had a lot of what if questions going through my head.

"Wassup what you want to talk about Juju?" Cree asked pulling me out of my thoughts.

"I just wanted to say sorry for what happened at the parking lot." I started off saying.

"Don't worry about it you made your bed and now you have to lay in it." Cree shrugged.

"What's that supposed to mean?"

"It means exactly what you think it means Juju. You had a nigga that was ready to give you the world and more but you picked the nigga that is only going to give you heart ache and heart break."

"You don't know what he is going to give me but I'm sure it's more than what you can offer." I said with an attitude.

"Yea whatever Juju. Just watch your nigga ight because everything isn't what it seems."

"Are you going to be straight forward or are you going to continue speaking in code." I asked sarcastically.

"It means do you know where your nigga is when you're not around?"

"Let me guess you know where he's at?"

"Nah I don't keep an eye on that nigga he's not my cup of tea. But I do know this he cheated on his chick with you and my mother always told me once a cheater always a cheater."

"How does that saying goes, takes a cheater to know a cheater."

"You are so childish Julani but you got that for now ma. I wish you nothing but the best." Cree said getting up and going back inside.

I shrugged off what he said and decided to go home. I would have stayed longer to chill with Phallyn but I didn't want to be around Cree right now. For some reason the words that Cree said were stuck in my head. He was right though I made my bed and now I had to lay in it hopefully it was the right bed that I made.

*****

"Messiah, where are you? When you get this message call me back please." I said leaving another voicemail.

I had been calling Messiah since I left Phallyn's house. He didn't pick up any of my phone calls. Everything that Cree was saying was starting to get to me. I picked up the phone to call him one last time and again he didn't answer. I threw my phone across the room not caring if it broke or not.

I was supposed to go to the club tonight but I just wasn't in the mood. I haven't been back there since everything happened. I was kind of embarrassed to show my face but I knew I would have to get over that sooner or later. I lay across my bed bored out of my mind when I heard my phone ringing. I almost fell off my bed trying to find where I threw my damn phone. I found it in one of my sneakers and picked it up without looking at the name on the screen.

"Hello" I said

"Julani what's wrong?" Messiah asked with urgency in his voice.

"Nothing is wrong but where the hell are you?"

"I'm out handling business doing what I have to do." He replied.

"What business are you handling Messiah and don't lie to me." I said annoyed.

"I'm about to go to the house and get the rest of my shit so I can move into the condo."

"I hope you know you're not going over there alone."

"Julani I don't need you coming along and starting drama. I'm just going to get my shit it's already packed I'ma be in and out."

"How do you know that your stuff is packed Messiah?"

"Why does it matter how I know that my stuff is packed?" Messiah sighed

"You've been talking to that bitch haven't you? I can't believe this shit." I said pissed the fuck off.

"Julani calm down I had to talk to her if I want to get my shit. Don't act dumb over this little shit, now just meet me at the condo."

"Nigga I'm not meeting you at the condo, I will meet you at the house you used to share with that bitch." I told him and hung up.

I quickly through on some sweats, a t-shirt and my sneakers. I went into my closet grabbed my .22 put it I my purse and was out the door. If Messiah thought I was just going to sit back and let him got to that house alone then he had another thing coming. I wasn't stupid I knew how females work; Amara wasn't going to let him go without a fight. A fight is exactly what she was going to get. Messiah didn't know that I was crazy and that I don't play about mine but he damn sure was going to learn today.

Chapter Twelve

I pulled up to the house that Amara and Messiah use to share ready for whatever. As I was walking up to the door I saw Messiah's car in the drive way. I put a little extra pep in my step so I could get to the door faster. I banged on the door like I was the police.

"Messiah you better bring your ass out here!" I yelled. I kept banging on the door until someone answered. The door flew open with Amara standing in the doorway with her arms crossed and a look of disgust on her face.

"What could you possibly want?" She asked with her nose turned up.

"Where is Messiah?"

"Damn y'all haven't even been together a full month and he got you doing pop up visits." Amara taunted.

"Bitch he don't got me doing anything. I just know how bitches like you work."

"Oh really then enlighten me how do bitches like me act?" she questioned.

"You're the needy type. You need for a nigga to take care of you because you can't take care of yourself. That's why it's so hard for bitches like you to let go of a nigga that doesn't want you." I shrugged.

"So let me tell you what type of bitch you are." Amara told me looking straight into my eyes. "You the worse type of bitch. You're the type of bitch that gets money and does everything for herself but can't get a nigga. You're the type of bitch that goes after someone else's nigga because you don't want to put in the work and effort to get your own. You think I'm with Messiah because I can't take care of myself? Well guess what, you're wrong. I was with that nigga because I love him. He was there for me when no one else was our relationship is a lot deeper than what meets the eye sweetie. Oh and as far as me letting go of Messiah, he's the one that came over here and let me suck his dick real quick. Why you think it took me so long to answer the door." Amara said rolling her eyes for emphasis.

"Messiah!" I yelled. My skin was boiling on the inside I couldn't believe that Amara had the nerve to tell me that shit. She was standing there with a smirk on her face like she had just won a prize. The more I looked at her, the more pissed off I got. In one quick motion I dropped my bag and slapped the shit out of her. I followed up the slap with a two piece combo and laid her ass out in her doorway.

"Messiah!" she called while trying to cover her face.

Her calling out for him like he was still her man had me seeing red. Every blow I threw was for every blow that she verbally delivered to my ego.

"Julani what the fuck are you doing." I heard Messiah say. He grabbed me into a bear hug pulling me off of Amara. He sat me down and fist started to fly, none of my punches were connecting but I didn't care because Messiah had me fucked up.

"You really gonna come to this bitches rescue but when I called your dumb ass you were acting like you were hard of hearing."

"Julani chill the fuck out!" Messiah demanded grabbing my arms.

"Nigga don't tell me to chill out when you the one over here getting your dick sucked. We only been doing this shit for two weeks and this is the type of bullshit you pull. I can't believe this shit Messiah; I really thought you were better than that. Two fucking weeks and you already out here acting like a hoe. Do you think that what my father told you about hurting me was a fucking game my nigga." I vented.

"Nobody cares about you and your daddy bitch. Shit you talk about me being needy when you need to look at yourself in the mirror" Amara said.

I yanked my arms out of Messiah's grasp and stormed over to my bag. I picked it up and pulled my gun out and pointed it at Amara. She quickly ran and stood behind Messiah.

"Bitch don't fucking run now you had all that fucking mouth a minute ago." I cried. My emotions were all over the place and I had these two mother fuckers to blame.

"Julani put the fucking gun down."

"You know what y'all two dumbasses aren't even worth it." I told them lowering the gun.

"Julani chill out and meet me at the condo ight." Messiah had the nerve to say.

"Messiah I know you're raggedy ass still don't want to be with this bitch?" Amara asked

"Watch your mouth."

I shook my head and ignored the both of them as I walked to my car. I got in and drove off with no sense of direction. I drove endlessly until I ended up at the condo. I didn't know why I came here after everything that had just happened but for some reason I did. I knew Messiah wasn't here yet so I decided to call Phallyn and tell her about this bullshit.

"Messiah ain't shit I should have just gave Cree a chance." I said as soon as I heard the phone stop ringing.

"I already told you Juju the bitch nigga wasn't what you wanted but you didn't wanna listen." Cree said.

"Cree?"

"The one and only."

"Why are you picking up Phallyn's phone?" I questioned.

"She left it here and I saw your name flash across the screen."

"Oh okay umm just tell her I called." I said slightly embarrassed that he heard my little confession.

"Nah let's talk you seem upset."

"I don't think that this is something that I can talk to you about." I didn't see the point in telling Cree what happened because the fact remained the same that I was stupid as hell to let him get away.

"I'm not going to force you to talk Juju but if you ever need someone to talk to I'm here." Cree said.

I was trying my hardest to hold in my smile but I couldn't. This was one of the things that I liked about Cree.

"Thanks Cree that means a lot especially after everything that happened between the both of us."

"I know I sounded salty about everything earlier but it's all love Juju."

"Who the fuck you talking to that got you smiling and shit!" Messiah yelled. I jumped just a little because I didn't see him walk up to my car.

"Cree I'll talk to you later ight." I said and hung up the phone before Cree could respond.

"Messiah don't walk up to my car questioning me about shit." I told him getting out the car.

"Just bring your ass in the house so we can talk." Messiah said walking away.

I reluctantly followed him in the house but made sure to slam the door behind me. I walked in the kitchen and jumped a little so I could sit on his counter. He walked over to me and tried to stand in between my legs but I pushed him away.

"Julani stop with the dumb shit ight." He said pushing my legs apart.

"You wanted to talk so talk."

"Stop looking so mean damn. You were just smiling a minute ago."

"Yea I was smiling because another nigga put it there and the sight of you wiped that smile right off my face."

"Julani don't get fucked up." he warned

"Nigga you don't get fucked up. You're the one out there getting your dick sucked by your supposed to be ex bitch. What is it Messiah she sucks your dick better than I do huh is that it."

"Julani don't even do that insecure shit ma because it ain't you. I let Amara suck my dick but that's all it was. She was coming on strong crying and doing the most so I gave in. She said it would give her closure."

"Nigga you can't be fucking serious. What makes you think her sucking your dick would give her closure. I know you're not that fucking stupid."

He shrugged his shoulders and as soon as his shoulders were relaxed I slapped the stupid out of him. As quickly as I smacked him he had his hand at my throat choking the shit out of me and this wasn't your normal rough you up choke; Messiah was dead ass choking me taking all the air out of lungs.

"Julani I don't play that hands shit okay, keep your hands to yourself and I'll do the same." He said letting me go.

I gasped for air and was trying to get my breathing under control. I had never seen Messiah get this aggressive and as odd as it sounded it turned me on.

"Messiah don't you ever put your fucking hands on me again." I told him taking a deep breath.

"Or what? What are you going to do Julani?" He said closing the little bit of space that was left between us.

We were starring each other in the eye and the sexually tension that filled the room was crazy. I leaned forward just a little and kissed him with all the passion that I could muster up. Our hands started to roam our bodies as we took turns ripping each other's clothes off. It didn't take long for Messiah to have me calling his name while bringing me to gut wrenching orgasms. What started as an argument ended in something that was so beautiful only lovers could understand.

Chapter Thirteen

How long you niggas ball? All day nigga. How much time you spent at the mall? All day nigga. How many runners do you got on call? All day nigga. Swish, swish. How long they keep you in court? All day nigga. Take you to get this fly? All day nigga. Tell your P.O. how long you been high? All day nigga. You already know I'm straight from the Chi, all day nigga. South, south, south side! All day nigga.

Kanye West's song All Day was blaring through the speakers in Allure. The club was packed from wall to wall and I couldn't have been happier. Phallyn and I were in the office talking about everything that happened yesterday after I left her house.

"You're better than me because I would have made his ass sweat a little before I let him hit it again. Oh and that Amara is a bold bitch." Phallyn laughed "I like her tho."

"What you mean you like her? Bitch you're my best friend, if I don't like someone neither do you." I said looking at her sideways.

"I'm not saying I'm buddy, buddy with the bitch. I'm just saying she bold she didn't back down from you in the parking lot and she read you when you went to her house all you can do is respect that. Plus what did you expect you took her fucking man."

I took a minute to think about what Phallyn had just said. Yeah Amara was bold and stood up for herself but that didn't mean that I respected her ass. There was no ring on Messiah's finger so he was fair game in my eyes it just so happen that I was the better woman because he chose me.

"Me taking Messiah from her isn't here nor there."

"Yea whatever. But where were you this morning I called you a couple of times to see if you wanted to go to breakfast."

"I was with Messiah."

"You were that busy with him that you couldn't pick up the phone." She asked giving me the side eye.

"You would think after having sex all night that he would be too tired to do it in the morning but this nigga is like the energizer bunny." I smiled. "You are so nasty. Y'all over there fucking like rabbits you better hope you don't end up pregnant."

"Would that be such a bad thing?"

"Julani don't even start, I know your ass isn't trying to get pregnant." She scolded

"I'm not trying to get pregnant but if it happens then it happens." I shrugged.

Before Phallyn could respond her phone started ringing. She answered it said a couple of words them hung up. From the smile on her face I could tell that it was Jacori who called her. "What you smiling for?" I asked.

"My baby just arrived" she said getting up. I followed her on to the elevator and over to the bar.

The only reason why I went with her was because I wanted to see if Cree was with Jacori. Even though things were cool between Messiah and me, I still wanted to keep Cree around as a friend. As we approached the bar I spotted Cree sitting next to Jacori looking fine as hell. I walked over and was about to give him a hug when some model looking broad walked in my way and stood in between his legs.

"Hey baby" the chick said above the music.

I repeated the words baby to myself because I couldn't believe this shit. Cree and I only stopped talking for three weeks and he already had a new bitch.

"Julani wassup." Jacori said.

"Hey Jacori" I said still eyeing Cree and his chick. It took me a minute to take my focus off of them but when I did I gave Jacori a hug.

I grabbed Phallyn by the arm so that I could whisper in her ear. "Who is that?"

"Some chick he messes with from what Jacori said it's nothing serious."

"And you didn't tell because?"

"I didn't feel like you needed to know. Why do you even care? You have Messiah isn't that the nigga that you wanted?"

I let go of Phallyn's arm and stormed away. Phallyn had a point but that didn't stop me from feeling some type of way. I went into the bathroom and looked at my appearance. I was dressed in a form fitting black dress with black gladiator heels. I pulled my hair down from the bun that it was in and let my curls hang free. I applied an extra coat of lip gloss and strutted out of the bathroom. I did my best model walk and strutted over to where Cree was and acted like the chick that was with him wasn't there.

"Hey Cree" I smiled "What are you doing here?"

"Juju wassup ma" he said pushing the model chick to the left a little so he could get up. The chick sucked her teeth as Cree gave me a hug.

We lingered in each other's embrace a little longer than we should have. I broke the hug and took a couple of steps back leaving a respectable amount of space between the two of us.

"Umm Cree who is this?" The female asked standing with her arms crossed.

"Tisha this is Julani she owns the club, Julani this is my friend Tisha." Cree introduced.

"Hey" I waved giving her a fake smile. I didn't care who the hell she was I just wanted to make my presence known.

"Yea Hi." She said dryly. "Cree I'm ready to go it's boring in here." She pouted.

"Yea Cree you better get her out of here before she dies of boredom." I replied sarcastically.

"It's not my fault you have a boring ass club." Tisha smirked.

I was about to respond when I felt a pair of arms wrap around my waist. I quickly spun around and came face to face with Messiah. He didn't look happy at all and he had his two boys with him Bones and Ty.

"Hey bae wassup." I asked trying to give him a kiss but he turned his face.

"Yo wassup I'm Messiah." Messiah said putting his hand out to Cree.

"Nigga I don't care to know you." Cree said ignoring Messiah's gesture.

"I was just trying to keep it civil because this is my shawty's place of business but we can most def take it there if you want to my nigga."

"Okay y'all need to chill with all of this." I said trying to diffuse the situation.

"Well Messiah I'm Tisha"

"Bitch that's all me right there and I don't play about mine. Just ask his last bitch." I told her ready to knock her head off.

"What's going on over here?" Phallyn asked walking over to us with Jacori not too far behind.

"Everything ight Cree?" Jacori asked mean mugging Messiah and his boys.

"Yea you know this bitch nigga don't put fear in my heart." Cree smirked getting up. "I'll see you later Julani." He said kissing me on the cheek before walking towards the exit.

The whole time Cree was walking out Messiah had his eyes locked on him mean mugging him. I didn't know what was about to pop off but I could tell that it was something.

"Julani I'll catch up with you later." Jacori said giving me a hug. "Phallyn let's go."

Before Phallyn followed Jacori out the door she gave me a hug and told me to call her. I was left standing with Messiah, Bones, Ty and Cree's chick that he had left.

"Let me talk to you in your office." Messiah asked

"Nah I'm okay I'm bout to go home, I have a doctor's appointment in the morning."

"It might have sounded like a request but it wasn't one." Messiah said taking step closer to me.

"Fine let's go." I told him with an attitude. Messiah grabbed my arm and led the way to my office.

I didn't want to have this conversation with Messiah because I felt like there wasn't anything to talk about. The person that he needed to talk to was Cree because Cree straight played his ass. I walked into my office and sat in my chair leaving Messiah standing at the door.

"What were you doing with dude?" Was the first thing that came out of his mouth.

"What do you mean what I was doing with him, I wasn't doing anything. He came to the club with Phallyn's boo so I went to the bar to say hi."

"I don't want you talking to that nigga."

"Who are you to tell me who I can and can't talk to?"

"Am I or am I not your dude?"

"Shit I can't tell." I said sarcastically.

"Julani don't be smart just answer the fucking question."

"Yea you're my dude."

"Ight then so don't talk to that nigga."

"You can't expect me to not talk to him when he's going to be around off of the fact that he's close with Phallyn's boo." I said trying to find every excuse so that I could still talk to him. Yeah Messiah was my dude but I still cared for Cree and wanted him around, I didn't know why I wanted to keep him I just did.

"I don't give a fuck you can stop talking to her too for all I care. But if I catch you talking to that nigga Julani there's going to be issues." He threatened.

"You got me fucked up if you think I'm going to stop talking to Phallyn for you. Phallyn's my best friend and nothing is going to get in the way of our friendship. As far as you wanting me to stop talking to Cree that's not going to happen until I know for sure that you ain't fucking Amara anymore."

"Man aint nobody fucking with that chick." Messiah said waving me off.

"But that's why you let her suck your dick right."

"I already explained that shit to you. Plus that's shit in the past so let it stay there."

"You didn't explain shit to me you gave me a bullshit ass excuse."

"Julani it is what it is. It's either you going to stop talking to the nigga or that's it for us."

"So that's how we are going to play. You know what fuck you Messiah I should have left your ass right with that bitch. You wanna leave me over me having a simple conversation with a nigga but you couldn't leave her because of the fucked up shit y'all went through together!" I yelled.

"Julani calm the fuck done and watch the tone of your voice!" Messiah yelled back.

"Nigga you watch the tone of your voice. Don't try to boss up now you should have said something to Cree when you called you're ass pussy."

I never realized how fast Messiah was until he had me pinned against the wall that was behind my desk. "You wanna throw that nigga in my face and shit Julani." He gritted

"Messiah get the fuck off me, I fucking hate your dumbass. I don't know why I went so hard to get you to begin with."

"You went so hard to get me because you love me. Now you herd what the fuck I said, if I catch you with that nigga I'll make sure that you never see him again." Messiah said. He kissed me roughly let me go and then walked out of my office.

I slid down the wall in office with tears in my eyes. Messiah was my fucking heart he meant the world to me but he also had the ability to break me. See I knew that I should have left Messiah's ass alone after Amara told me that she sucked his dick but my dumb ass stayed and gave him some pussy. The love that I had for Messiah was unconditional and when you love someone that deep you overlook the bad that they do because you hoped that things would change. Then on the other hand we had Cree. The chemistry that we shared whenever we were in the same room spoke volumes but that didn't matter because my heart belonged to Messiah. It was crazy though because when I saw Cree with that girl I felt a rush of jealousy go through my body and it had me second guess how I felt.

My phone started ringing pulling me out of my thoughts. I looked down at the screen and saw my father's number flashing across the screen.

"Hello" I answered the phone wiping my tears away.

"Juju are you okay? Why do you sound like you're crying?" My father asked sounding concerned.

"I'm OK daddy but wassup?"

"I called because I was about to leave to go on a business trip when a friend of yours came knocking on the door asking for you."

"A friend of mine, daddy I don't know who you are talking about."

"He said his name is Cree."

"Cree" I repeated. What the hell was he doing there I thought.

"Yea do you know him?"

"Uh yea I know him his friend dates Phallyn. I'm bout to be on my way to the house now."

"Well hurry up and get here because you know I don't like when random people pop up at the house especially late at night. You know I don't play that shit and I will go 180 real quickly." My father said hanging up the phone.

I jumped up off the floor and rushed out of the club. I didn't know what Cree was trying to pull but he didn't know my father. I got in my car and sped home to find out what the fuck was going on. It just seemed like my night was getting better and better by the minute.

Chapter Fourteen

I rushed into the house to find Cree and my father laughing it up in the living room.

"What's so funny?" I asked making my presence known.

"Nothing your father was just telling me a joke." Cree said.

"So what are you doing here?" I asked Cree with a raised eyebrow.

"I came to talk to you."

"Okay we can go into my room to talk." I said

Cree got up and walked over to me so we could head up to my bedroom but my dad stopped us.

"Cree go on up I need to talk to my daughter before I leave."

"It's upstairs and the third door to the right." I told Cree.

I went over to the couch where Cree was sitting and sat down. I looked over at my father and he had a worried look on his face. His eyes kept going from my face to my stomach.

"Daddy what's the matter why do you keep looking at me like that?"

"Julani Marie Cortez are you pregnant?" My father asked out of nowhere.

"Where the hell did you get that from?"

"Just answer the questions Julani are you pregnant?"

"No not that I know of." I answered honestly

"Make a doctor's appointment tomorrow and let me know what happens."

"I already have one. But what makes you think that I'm pregnant. I haven't had morning sickness or food cravings."

"Julani those are not the only signs of pregnancy. Just let me know what happens at the appointment tomorrow. I'm going to Miami for a couple of weeks and while I'm gone I need you to be in charge of everything. You don't have to touch anything I just need you to make sure that people are confirming that they got their work and that they have my money. Everything else is set up for you." My father told me.

"Okay daddy. Be safe and I love you."

"I love you too and don't forget to let me know what happens."

I gave my father a hug and helped him with his bags to the door. I waited until he got in his car and pulled off before I went upstairs to find out what Cree wanted. I walked up the stairs leading to my bedroom thinking about what my father said about me being pregnant. There could have been a possibility that I was pregnant but I wasn't showing any signs of pregnancy. I quickly pushed the thought out of my mind and walked into my room. Cree was laid out across my bed looking like he was about to go to sleep.

"Cree what are you doing here?" I asked slipping out of my heels.

"I wanted to talk to you." He said sleepily

"Well hurry up and talk because I have an appointment in the morning and I'm tired as hell."

"I'll wait until you get comfortable." Cree said watching me as I undressed.

I slipped the dress over my head and looked in my draw for a t-shirt. When I found one I put it on and sat in my lazy boy chair that was in the corner of my room.

"Okay talk I'm comfortable." I said

"Your dad is a cool dude."

"I know you didn't come here to talk about my father."

"No I didn't but I'm just saying that he and I could be real cool one day you know."

"I doubt it. Now what do you want to talk about. Don't you have Tisha to go home to?"

"Julani are you jealous?" Cree laughed.

"No I'm not jealous I have no reason to be. She doesn't have anything that I want." I lied

"Yea right you know you want me which is why you came back over to the bar tonight to make your presence known."

"Cree I don't want you I'm perfectly fine with Messiah."

"So where the nigga at then. You came home alone instead of with your nigga." Cree smirked.

"Cree I'm not having this conversation with you."

"Julani stop lying to yourself, as much as you love that nigga you're not happy with him."

"Why do you care if I'm happy or not. You obviously moved on real quick with that Tisha bitch." I said sounding every bit of jealous.

"That's not my girl I was just fucking her until you came to your sense."

"Came to my senses about what. I don't know how many times I have to tell you that I'm in love with Messiah."

"If you were in love with that nigga you wouldn't be entertaining this conversation. Julani you're mine whether you like it or not. But the sooner you realize it the better everyone else is going to be."

"Cree I'm not yours I will never be yours. Maybe if we were in another life time and Messiah wasn't around; then maybe we might've had a shot but that's not the case."

"Julani come here." Cree said sitting up on the bed.

I reluctantly walked over to him and pulled me on to his lap. "Cree what do you want?" I asked acting like I was annoyed but I was enjoying this whole thing.

"I want you to give us a chance. Julani I know what you need and it's not that nigga that you trying to play house with."

Looking into Cree's eyes I wanted to give in and tell him that I would take a chance on him but I just couldn't do that to Messiah.

"Cree I can't do that. I wish I could but I can't the way I feel for him…" My sentence was cut off from Cree kissing me.

I tried my hardest not to give into the kiss but I couldn't deny the passion between us. I gave in and let my tongue dance around his. Kissing Cree felt different then kissing Messiah, with Cree there was passion and chemistry, with Messiah there was just lust.

"Julani I know you felt that but look I'm going to give you a week to get your shit together and let ole boy know that you aint fucking with him anymore."

"Cree I don't know if I can do that." I told him being honest.

"It's not up for discussion you got a week to let him know that your mine ight. But for now come lay down I'm spending the night with you."

I allowed Cree to pull me into his arms and I nestled into his chest. My mind was racing trying to figure out what my next move was. Even though I wasn't in love with Cree the way that I felt when I was in his presence spoke volumes compared to how I felt when I was with Messiah. Whenever Messiah and I were around each other it was more of a sexual thing, maybe I was confusing love with lust. I fell asleep trying to figure out whom I wanted to be with and if what I felt for Messiah was real.

Chapter Fifteen

"Julani wake up your alarm is going off." Cree said shaking me.

I reached over to grab my phone but it slipped out my hand. Cree ended up having to reach around me and pick it off the floor and turn it off.

"Julani get up you're going to miss you appointment." Cree said.

"Just five more minutes please." I yawned.

"I have something that can wake your ass up." Cree said rubbing my thigh.

It didn't take me long to figure out what he was talking about. I got right out of bed and went to my closet to look for something to wear. After the last time Cree and I had sex I was feeling like a thot so I made a promise to myself that I wouldn't sleep with Cree again unless we were together.

"I knew that would get your ass up, you ain't ready for another round with me." Cree smirked.

"Please I handled you very well last time and I'm pretty sure I can handle you again." I told him.

"Want to test that theory of yours?"

"Nah I'm good I have a doctor's appointment to go to." I smiled.

"Uh huh, you want me to come with you?" he asked sitting up in bed.

"You can come if you want. It's going to be boring though."

"Nothing is boring when I'm with you."

"Yea whatever" I laughed. "Do you have something else to put on?" Cree still had on the outfit that he was wearing the night before at the club.

"Yea I got some extra clothes in my car."

"Ok so you can shower in my bathroom and I'll go use my father's. Everything that you might need is in the linen closet right next to the bathroom okay."

He nodded his head and I left out the room so that I could hurry and shower. I didn't have time to take long shower like I wanted to. I quickly washed up, rinsed off and got out all within twenty minutes. I wrapped my robe around me and decided to go get a glass of juice before I went into my room. I walked in the kitchen and noticed that my front door was open. I walked over to the door to see why Cree would leave it open and saw him and Messiah in what looked to be like a heated conversation.

Without even thinking I ran outside with nothing on but a robe and my hello kitty slippers. "What the hell is going on?" I asked standing in between them.

"Julani what the fuck is this nigga doing here and why you out here in a fucking robe." Messiah said

"Nigga don't be questioning her and watch your tone." Cree said coming to my defense.

"I can talk to my bitch however I fucking feel like."

"Messiah I know you upset but don't call me out my fucking name." I told him. "Cree just go back in the house please and let me handle this.

Cree looked Messiah up and down smirked and then started to walk towards the house. I waited to see if he was going to go inside but his ass stayed right in the door way. I shook my head and turned my attention back to Messiah.

"Messiah what are you even doing here?" I questioned him.

"I came over to apologize to you for what happened last night but I can see your hoe ass is already busy and moved on to the next nigga."

"Hoe who you calling a hoe. Messiah you got me all the way fucked up!" I yelled

"Nah I think I got you just right, I should have known what type of bitch that you were from how you came on to me while I was with Amara."

"Really Messiah is that really what you think of me?" I asked hurt that he would think I was like that. Regardless of how it looked he should have known me better than that.

"Man I don't know what to think. But you can finish playing house with home boy I'm out." Messiah said walking away

"So that's it you just going to walk away you're not even going to let me explain." I cried.

"There is nothing for you to explain ma the proof is in the pudding." He shrugged and got in his car. I watched him as he pulled out of my drive way and I collapsed to the floor. Tears were flooding down my eyes and I didn't care.

"Julani get you're naked ass up. You out here crying and shit over that nigga." Cree said walking over to me. He scooped me up in his arm and I cried into his shoulder like I was a big ass baby.

"Julani you really crying over that nigga?" Cree asked again.

"How would you feel if you were him and you saw another dude coming out your girl's house and then your girl comes out wearing nothing but a robe?"

"I can't answer that."

"Exactly because you know you would feel the same way that he does."

"Nah I can't answer that because I wouldn't leave any room for another nigga to try and slide his way in. I'm telling you Juju Messiah don't deserve your ass and like I told you before you're mine so dry them eyes and go get dressed so we can be out." Cree said sitting me down on the bed.

I waited until he went in the bathroom to get dressed because I didn't want him to see my tear stained face. Messiah leaving like he did and me crying confirmed what I was so confused about last night. I was indeed in love with Messiah.

*****

"Ms. Cortez how are you today." My doctor asked walking into the room.

"I'm okay I guess." I shrugged.

"Well today as you know we are going to do a regular routine. So if you could fill up this cup that would be great." She said handing me a plastic cup. I went into the bathroom and filled the cup up instantly. I washed my hands before I went back in the room with the doctor. I hand her the cup of pee and sat back up on the chair.

"Umm is it possibly that you can do a pregnancy test" I shyly asked.

"You're pregnant?" The doctor asked.

"Not that I know of but my father wants me to get one."

"Well parents always know best I'll run one for you and also give you an ultrasound just give me a couple of minutes."

The doctor left the room and I felt like I was sitting in the office forever. My cellphone vibrated I looked down at it and it was a text from Phallyn asking what I was doing for the day. I told her that I was at the doctor's office and that I would catch up with her later. I started to doze off when I heard Cree call my name.

"Cree what are you doing back here?"

"I got bored waiting for you out there. Is everything okay, you been back here for a minute."

"Yea everything is fine I'm just waiting for the doctor to run a test for me."

"Ight well she needs to hurry up a nigga is hungry." Cree said rubbing his stomach.

"I'm hungry too now that you mention it. I can go for some pancakes from Ihop."

"Ight then that's where we'll go as soon as you finish." Cree smiled.

I smiled back at him just as the doctor was walking back in the room. She was looking at papers that were on her clip board. I was nervous as hell for her to tell me if I was pregnant or not only because Cree was now in the room.

"Oh is this your boyfriend." The doctor asked finally looking away from the clip board.

"Yes I am my name is Cree."

"Well nice to meet you Cree or should I say daddy." The doctor smiled.

"What you mean daddy? Who's pregnant?" Cree asked

The smile the doctor had on her face began to fade "Uh Ms. Cortez is pregnant." The doctor said unsure if she should have shared the information.

"Do you know how far along I am?" I asked just out of curiosity.

"Not yet but I can find out, if you don't mind lift up your shirt for me please."

I did as the doctor said and lifted up my shirt; I watched as she squirted this blue gel on my stomach and rolled the transducer over my stomach.

"If you look at the screen you can see the little embryo that will later on be your baby." The doctor said.

I looked over at the screen and instantly fell in love. Even though my baby was just a little egg I still felt a connection to it.

"So how many weeks is she doc?" Cree asked.

"From the looks of it she is about two weeks or three weeks. I'm going to go ahead and clean you up and then give you a couple of prescriptions." The doctor said.

She wiped the blue gel off my stomach and then went back to her clip board. I looked over at Cree and he looked like he was deep in thought.

"Here you go." The doctor said handing me three prescriptions. "Get these filled as soon as you can and I'll see you back here in the next two weeks."

I thanked the doctor gathered my things and walked out the hospital as quickly as I could. I couldn't believe that I was pregnant but what made it even worse was that I didn't know exactly who the father was. If I was four or five weeks it could be Messiah's or Cree's because I slept with the both of them back to back. I got in the car and couldn't wait to call Phallyn so that I could vent to her.

Cree was quiet the whole car ride which was fine with me because I was too damn shocked to talk.

I had way too many thoughts going through my head. I didn't know how I was going to tell Messiah that I was pregnant and that the baby might not be his.

"You know we gonna have to talk about this right?" Cree said looking at me from the corner of his eye.

"I know Cree but I need time." I sighed

"Is it a possibility that the baby could be mine."

"Yea" I whispered. I watched him run his hand over his face and instantly felt like shit.

"Can you drop me off at Phallyn's house?" He nodded his head yeah and didn't say anything else.

*****

When he pulled up in front of Phallyn's building I went to get out the car when he stopped me. I turned around to look at him and all I saw was love in his eyes.

"Julani regardless of whose baby it is I'm still gonna be there. This little problem doesn't change anything. Remember what I said you got a week."

"Okay." I whispered and got out the car.

I walked inside Phallyn's building without looking back. I climbed the few flights of stairs up to Phallyn's apartment and knocked on the door.

"Julani what's the matter." Phallyn asked when she opened the door and saw the tears rolling down my face.

I walked into her apartment and flopped right on the couch, I was feeling like my world was over.

"Julani what's the problem you're scaring me."

"I'm pregnant."

"Say word."

"Word."

"Damn when did you find out?" Phallyn asked sitting next to me rubbing my back.

"Today when I went to the doctor with Cree."

"Wait why was Cree with you?" She asked confused

"When I got home last night he was there waiting for me. He said he wanted to talk."

"Well did y'all talk?"

"We talked he basically said that I was his and that I had a week to let Messiah know. Then this morning when we were getting ready to go to the doctors Messiah pops up and him and Cree get into it. Like you just don't understand all this stress that I have going on in my life right now."

"I can't say that I understand what you're going through because I don't but a lot of the shit you're going through is because of you."

I looked at Phallyn like she had just lost her mind. "Phallyn what do you mean this is my fault? I didn't ask to get pregnant and I damn sure didn't ask for all this drama that's been coming my way."

"Julani please stop playing the victim. You were the one that was having unprotected sex with the both of them. As far as everything else if you weren't so damn jealous and felt like Messiah was supposed to be yours then you wouldn't have half the drama that you have now."

"I can't fucking believe this shit I come over here to vent because I'm upset and I have to get told that everything is my fault."

"Julani I'm not saying that everything is your fault I'm just saying that you caused a lot of the drama in your life and now that you're having a baby you need to change a couple of things about yourself."

"What could I possibly have to change with myself?" I was getting upset with the direction that this conversation was going in. All I wanted was for Phallyn to listen to my issues and tell me that everything was going to be alright. I didn't need a lecture because I already knew once I told my father what was going on I would have to hear it from him too.

"This is me being honest with you Juju. You are lost in love and it's not a good look for you. You let Messiah get away with murder and word on the street is Amara is pregnant. You should have left his ass alone when he let that hoe suck his dick."

The only thing I heard was that Amara was pregnant. "Where did you hear that Amara is pregnant?"

"It doesn't matter where I heard it the point is that I heard. See this is what I mean you worried about the wrong shit. Yeah the fact that Amara might be pregnant is fucked up but you need to move on. I been telling you from the jump that this nigga wasn't right for you but you too damn hard headed to listen."

"So fucking what if I didn't listen to you I listened to my heart which is all that matters. You should have been told me this shit because I'm sure that you just didn't hear this shit."

"You're right I didn't just hear it I heard back when we wasn't talking for two week. But don't put this off on me like it's my fault."

"It's not your fault but you could have told me."

"At some point you have to learn for yourself and this is one of them times. I love you Julani and whatever you decide to do I will be here for you but I can't stand by and watch you waste your time with Messiah."

"Thanks a lot for the support." I said sarcastically. I got up and left her apartment without saying anything else. Phallyn was supposed to be there for me no matter what and the time I needed her most she wants to try and give me tough love.

I walked out of her building forgetting that I had Cree drop me off. I pulled my phone out to call cab. The cabbie said that he would be here in ten minutes so I decided to sit on the steps. I sat there trying not to think about all the hell that had been going on in my life. I knew that the only way I was going to figure all this shit out is if I talked to Messiah. I needed to talk to him and find out if there was any truth to Amara being pregnant. I looked at my phone and scrolled through my call log until I came across his name. I pressed the call button and patiently waited until he picked up the phone. He didn't pick up so I called back a couple more times, after the fourth phone call I left him a message.

"Messiah I need to talk to you its important call me back." I listen to the playback and then hung up the phone. My phone started to ring and I almost got excited until I saw that it was the number for the cab.

"Hello."

"You're cab is coming down the street."

"Okay thank you." I said and hung up the phone. I got up off the steps and jumped into the cab. I gave the guy my address and stared out the window as he pulled off. I didn't want to be bothered at all unless it was Messiah calling me back.

Chapter Sixteen

I turn my cheek music up and I'm puffing my chest. I'm getting ready to face you, can call me obsessed. It's not your fault that they hover I mean no disrespect. It's my right to be hellish I still get jealous. 'Cause you're too sexy, beautiful and everybody wants a taste that's why I still get jealous.

I was in the bed trying to fall asleep when I heard my phone going off. It was playing Nick Jonas song Jealous which is the ringtone I set for Messiah. I was happy that he was calling back but pissed off at how long it took him.

"Hello" I said answering the phone.

"Fuck Messiah" I heard someone moan.

"Hello." I said again. Nobody answered but I could hear people talking in the background.

"Amara you don't ever have to worry I'ma always be there for you and the baby." Messiah groaned.

"Mhmmm you love this pussy don't you baby."

"Hell yea."

"Tell me you love me daddy so I can come all over this dick." Amara hissed.

"I love you baby." I heard Messiah say and I hung up the phone.

I sat in the bed stunned at what I just heard. This bitch was really pregnant by my fucking man and my so called man was over there telling that bitch he loved her like I didn't blow up his phone earlier. Tears started to fall down my face but I quickly wiped them away. Messiah and Amara done fucked with the wrong one and I was going to show them just who the fuck Julani Marie Cortez was.

I got out of bed turned on my light and quickly found something to wear. I wanted to call Phallyn so she could ride out with me but seeing how things went earlier I figured this would be better if I went alone. I grabbed my .22 out my purse and my car keys and was headed to the door. I was moving so fast that I walked right into Cree's chest at the front door.

"Julani where are you going in a rush and why are you dressed like you 'bout to body someone." Cree laughed.

"I have to go handle something." I told him locking the door.

"Then I'm going with you." Cree said jumping in the passenger seat.

"Cree I don't need you coming with me I'm a big girl I can handle this." I told him.

"I don't know what you are trying to handle but I do know you're pregnant with a baby that could possibly be mine."

"Thanks for reminding me." I said

I pulled my iPod out of the glove compartment and scrolled until I found Trey Songz Smartphone. I hit the play button hooked it up to the speakers in my car and pulled off. While Trey Songz was singing about lying to his chick's face tears were flowing down mines. I was heart broke but most of all pissed off because my father and Phallyn were right. They both told me that Messiah wasn't shit but my dumb ass didn't want to listen and now I had to find out the hard way.

"Julani, why you listening to this depressing ass song?" Cree asked turning it down.

"Cree now is not the time." I told him keeping it short.

"Let me guess it has something to do with that other nigga. What he do now, did he call you by accident and you heard him having sex." Cree laughed.

I looked at him with the deadliest look that I could muster up causing his laughter to fade.

"Julani you can't be serious he really did that shit? Man I already told you that nigga wasn't bout shit."

Ignoring the little that Cree had to say, I drove right on to the grass that was outside of Amara's house. I got out with my gun in hand and start banging on the front door. Nobody was answering the door fast enough for me. I searched their yard for a big enough rock, when I found one I picked it up and threw it right through the window. It was around 4 in the morning and I was out here acting like a mad woman but I honestly didn't care because if I was heartbroken then that bitch had to be heartbroken too.

"What the fuck!?" I heard Messiah yell from the inside.

"Messiah bring your dog ass out here now!" I yelled.

"Julani what are you doing here and why the fuck you throwing shit through my windows." Messiah yelled coming outside.

"Fuck you and these windows. You didn't see my four missed calls."

"You out here acting up over missed calls? Man go ahead with that bullshit." Messiah said dismissing me.

"Nah I came over here to tell your bitch congratulations." I smirked.

"Oh bae you told her the good news? Or did you get me little phone call?" Amara said coming outside and standing next to Messiah like he was some type of prized possession. The sight of those two made me fucking sick to my stomach.

"Yea I got your little phone call but guess what bitch. You aren't the only one that's pregnant."

"Messiah what the fuck is she talking about?" Amara said hitting Messiah in the arm.

"Oh he didn't tell you we sister wives now bitch, you ain't ever going to get rid of me." I yelled charging towards Amara. Messiah grabbed me and pushed me back causing me to fall on the ground.

"My nigga you put your hands on the wrong one" Cree said walking towards us. This nigga was so quiet that I forgot that he was even here.

"Juju come get your bitch boy before I lay his ass out and put him six feet under." Messiah said getting in Cree's face.

Before I could intervene Cree punched him in the face and the two of them started to go at it. I took a step back and just looked at all the chaos that I caused all because I was jealous of what another woman had. I shook my head and started walking back to my car because I was truly embarrassed by the whole thing. I looked back one last time at Messiah and Cree fighting before I got in my car and drove off.

Chapter Seventeen

It has been two days' since I went over to Amara's house acting a fool. The only person that I was talking to was my father. I had both Cree and Messiah blowing my phone up but I refused to take either one of their calls. Phallyn had stopped by my house a couple of times to check on me but I was keeping her at arm's length too. I had too much going on in my life right now and I just didn't want to be bothered with anyone. For the past two days I kept replaying what happened over and over in my head. I couldn't believe that I acted that way and it was all over a dude that really didn't want me to begin with.

"Julani open the door." I heard Messiah yell outside.

I got off the living room couch and looked out the window to see Messiah standing there with a bouquet of roses. I didn't want to answer the door for him but I still had a soft spot for him. I reluctantly opened the door and allowed him to come in.

"Messiah what do you want." I sighed

"Can we at least sit and talk."

"No we can stay right here because you won't be staying long."

"I just want to say sorry for everything that happened the other day. I never meant for you to find out about Amara that way and after you left I told her that we were done for good."

"That's nice to know Messiah but I honestly don't care."

"Julani don't say that. We have a baby together we can make this work." He said caressing my cheek.

"This baby might not even be yours" I told him pushing his hand away.

"What do you mean it might not be mine? Who the fuck baby could it be?" He yelled.

Messiah had this crazed look in his eye that made me a little nervous. I took a couple steps back but he yanked me by the collar of my shirt.

"Messiah please let me go." I begged.

"You let that nigga fuck you Julani? You're trying to tell me that the baby could be his." Messiah said pulling a gun out from his waist.

"Messiah what are you doing?" I asked nervously.

"Julani I hope you don't think that I'm just going to sit back and let you carry another nigga's seed." Messiah said with tears in his eyes.

He shoved me against the wall and pointed the gun at my stomach. I closed my eyes scared for my life and for my unborn child's life. I heard the gun go off and then felt the sting as the bullet ripped through me. I fell to the floor with tears in my eyes; I couldn't believe that Messiah had just shot me. People always said that jealous was the ugliest trait I guess I understood why now.....

To Be Continued.....

Contact Me

Facebook: Kellz Kimberly

Instagram: Kellzkimberlyxoxo

Snapchat: Kellzkayy

Website: Kellzkinc.com

CPSIA information can be obtained
at www.ICGtesting.com
Printed in the USA
LVOW12s1814011016
507014LV00001B/269/P

9 781537 496818

Dick Sutphen's
Enlightenment
Transcripts

Valley of the Sun Publishing, Box 38, Malibu, CA 90265

Dick Sutphen's
Enlightenment
Transcripts

For information on Sutphen Seminars, Dick's tapes and a free copy of his magazine, write: Dick Sutphen, Box 38, Malibu, California 90265

Other Valley of the Sun Books by Dick Sutphen

Poetry
Rattlesnake Karma (1985)—$5.95
Poet-Anthology 1970-1985 (1985)—$5.95

Psychic/Metaphysical
The Master of Life Manual (1980/1986)—$3.95
Past-Life Therapy In Action (1983)—$2.95
Sedona: Psychic Energy Vortexes (1986)—$7.95

General
Assertiveness Training & How To Instantly
Read People (1978/1983)—$2.95

First Printing: September, 1986

Additional copies of **Enlightenment Transcripts** are available by mail for $3.95 each. Send check or money order, plus $1.50 per order postage, to: Valley of the Sun Publishing, Box 38, Malibu, California 90265. The companion volume to this book is **The Master of Life Manual,** which explores many additional concepts. We also suggest **Past-Life Therapy In Action** by Dick Sutphen and Lauren Leigh Taylor.

Cover Photography by Dick Sutphen—
Clouds and ocean: The Florida Keys
Seagull and ocean: Malibu, California

Library of Congress Catalog Card Number: 86-050990
ISBN: 0-87554-055-4

4

To my wife,
Tara

*O*ur goal is to transform
the restrictive thinking
of mankind into
self-actualized awareness
which will manifest
a New Age of
peace, light and love.

Section One
The Courage To Live Dangerously

This book is a condensed overview of the teachings found in my other books, seminars and many audio tapes. The dialogues between participants and myself were taken from tape recordings of **Bushido** and **Master of Life Training** Seminars conducted in various cities throughout the country. Notes taken at the seminars were also used to recreate accurate interactions. The names have been changed, and in some situations, dialogues have been combined or edited to avoid repetition.

The seminars consist of short, powerful talks, altered-state-of-consciousness explorations and processing sessions. Participants are always invited to question or share their experiences. They may raise their hand to interact with me if they desire, but there is no pressure to share individually. I do encourage everyone attending to leap into the unknown to find their True Selves. The True Self is found when the false self is renounced. To accomplish that goal, I must jolt those attending out of their intellectual ruts, passé notions, views and convictions that are restricting their lives.

9

Outside the seminar room setting, some of the communications may appear cold and unfeeling to a reader. In reality, they are a form of the Zen teacher/student association, and I have only one goal in mind: to create the space for the participant to help himself by finding his own truths. And I must do this even at the cost of incurring his dislike.

The search for **true freedom** is what all of my communications are ultimately about—freedom **of** the self and **from** the self. Freedom **of** the self means literal freedom; freedom from oppressive environments and relationships, the freedom of a satisfying career, and the freedom to make your life meaningful. Freedom **from** the self is the path that leads to supreme enlightenment—to becoming a Master. This is the freedom which allows you to rise above all fears and to express unconditional love.

1.
Arlene

A pretty woman in her late thirties raised her hand, indicating that she wanted to ask a question. I pointed to her. She stood up and said, "I really don't have any major problems, but life just isn't very fulfilling. My husband and I get along all right and we both have good jobs, so why do I feel so ... so uninspired?"

I responded by saying, "You aren't experiencing any aliveness, Arlene."

"What is aliveness?" she asked.

"Aliveness is excitement, enjoyment in doing what you do. It's that blood-pumping exhilaration, challenge, joy, stimulation and pleasure that makes life worth living."

"You're right," she said, looking at the floor. "There certainly isn't much aliveness in my life now. But there used to be."

"When was that?" I asked.

"Oh, lots of times. I think I've known my share of excitement and stimulation. When I was a child, of course. But also early in my relationship with Frank. We shared plenty of great times. And when he and I were starting our business, we had more challenge than we knew what to do with."

"But now your relationship and career are secure and it's boring, right?"

"Right!" she responded.

"Welcome to what is, Arlene. Somewhere around the age of 35 and on, people begin to burn out. Eventually, they just run on the momentum they have generated up until that point in their life. It's like riding a bicycle. You have to pump and pump and work at it to get up to speed, but then the momentum will carry you for a while without much effort.

"Eventually, no matter how you make your living, your career gets boring. If you remain in the same job or career to make the payments and fulfill your obligations, sooner or later it all becomes work. The reward for your success just seems to be frustration."

"That's exactly it," Arlene said, raising her hands in a gesture of futility.

"And now you're just looking for places to hide, aren't you?" I asked.

"I don't understand what you mean," she replied.

"Places to hide, to fill your time. Many people just become couch potatoes and sit in front of their TV sets every night. I see a lot of people get involved in what I call 'cosmic foo-foo.' This is the spooky spirituality that gets your attention but offers little in the way of enlightenment. Excessive gossiping with friends is a great place to hide. Anything you are doing that doesn't offer growth or fulfillment is a place to hide."

Arlene didn't verbally respond, but shook her head knowingly while glancing up and to the left. (This is a

11

neurolinguistic indicator that she was remembering images.)

"You see, you have to do something to keep life from getting too dull, boring and mundane. Your mind can't handle boredom. In fact, if life does become too boring, your mind will subconsciously create something to make your life more interesting. It might generate sickness—a kidney stone would give you something to talk about, wouldn't it? Or maybe your mind would create a tragic accident.

"Often people die shortly after retirement, not because they need to, but because life becomes so boring that their minds can't handle it. That's the way energy works. And people are energy. Albert Einstein discovered that matter is energy. Matter appears solid, but in reality it is vibrating molecules of energy. Your mind is energy. Your body is energy. Your soul is energy, and the only difference between them is their vibrational rate."

"Yeah, and my energy is definitely down," Arlene blurted.

"That's a more accurate statement than you probably realize," I said. "Physicists have proven that energy doesn't die. It can't, it must go somewhere. It merely changes composition or structure. And since you are energy, you can't die; you simply transform, or reincarnate, in a new form. But scientists have also proven that energy never stands still. It either moves forward, expanding, or it moves backward, dissipating ... and preparing to transform itself."

"Oh, great!" Arlene said loudly. "Are you saying I'm in the process of dissipating and preparing to transform, which probably means getting ready to die and be reborn?"

"Possibly! You just told me that your life is boring and uninspired. It depends on how far you let that go. Numerous medical research projects have proven that

12

the more uninvolved and uninspired an individual is, the greater the possibility that person will get sick."

"So you're saying aliveness, as you call it, causes energy to move forward and expand?" Arlene asked.

"Exactly!"

"Okay, but realistically, what can you do to create aliveness and still be responsible to your existing life, relationship and career?" she asked, her hands now planted assertively on her hips.

"My first suggestion is **challenge**, Arlene. Challenge always generates energy. Challenge is essential to your well-being. People need challenge in their lives. If they don't have it, eventually they do something to create it, as I've already said, be it sickness, an accident, an affair, bankruptcy or whatever. Of course, some choose to die instead, but most of us just destroy what we have because there is no longer any challenge. Then we have the challenge to rebuild, and life becomes exciting again. Aliveness returns."

"Oh, come on," Arlene snapped. "I'm not going to destroy what I have so I can have the challenge of rebuilding it."

"No, consciously you won't ... but subconsciously, you will begin to draw circumstances to you which will generate solutions leading you back to aliveness. Look at your own life, and the lives of your friends and associates; look at history. Historically, a country that has reached its peak becomes stagnant when it experiences no more challenges, fragmenting and finally collapsing entirely. I'm sure you know couples who struggled through adversity until things finally began to go well. And that's when they got their divorce. When there is no challenge, stagnation begins, and stagnation is self-destruction because energy can't stand still. It must, by its very nature, be in constant motion—whether forward or backward."

13

"So, I need to create challenges in my life?" Arlene said, almost distantly.

"I don't know, Arlene. Do you?"

"I think so, " she replied, sitting down.

2.
Beth & John

"I don't buy what you just said to Arlene. I've got more challenge in my life than I can deal with, but I am not excited about it. There is certainly no joy or pleasure or aliveness in it."

"All right, Beth, let's explore your situation. You're dressed quite formally to be attending this rather casual seminar. Yesterday, you were dressed just as formally, although you certainly must have observed the attire of the other participants," I said.

"What in the world does that have to do with anything?" she snapped.

"It says to me that you are very concerned with projecting the image of a proper lady, Beth."

"Of course I am! Since when is there anything wrong with that?" she said, now obviously angry.

"There is nothing wrong with it. Society in general certainly approves and I have no doubt you'd win the 'Best Dressed' award if we had a contest here today. It's just that, to me, your attire says you are a phony."

"What?" she screamed, picking up her purse, preparing to walk out of the seminar. "I should have known better than to come to a gathering like this."

"Beth, is one of your life patterns to leave every time things aren't going your way? In relationships, in your career . . . with friends?" She stopped in the aisle, having moved down her row of seated participants. I continued, "Stay for once, Beth. You just might learn something valuable about yourself."

"The idea that you could teach me anything valuable is a joke," she snapped bitterly, remaining in the aisle.

"There is nothing personal in my remark, Beth. Look at John over there in his expensive, dark blue suit, white shirt and maroon tie. He looks like he's ready to deliver the NBC Nightly News, or attend an oil company board meeting. He's also a phony. There's nothing personal in it ... it's just what is."

Now John stood, also upset with me. "Just a minute, Beth," he said. "Let's complete this, then I'll go with you." He then turned his attention back to me and said, "What does this have to do with Beth's original question? We paid to come here to learn from you, not to be insulted about how we dress. You obviously didn't care enough about your attire to bother. You look to me like you're ready to go to the beach, not conduct a professional seminar." (My attire was a denim sportcoat, a 1986 Great Peace March T-shirt, faded Levis and white running shoes.)

"Okay, John and Beth, let go of your anger for just a moment and let me use this situation to make a few points. Obviously, I now have everyone's attention. First, Beth, tell me what statement my clothing makes to you."

Beth hesitated a moment, then said, "Well, between your long hair and your clothing, I get that you don't much care what anyone thinks."

"I think you're wrong, Beth," John said. "I think he cares just as much as you and I do about the image he projects. He doesn't want to be mistaken as a part of the establishment. Like it or not, he is expressing what he is, and he is going to say we are hiding what we are. And so what?"

"What about that?" I asked. They both just stared at me for several seconds, then John spoke. "I won't speak for myself, but Beth fits into society a lot better than

15

anyone else in this room. She is wearing an expensive suit and she obviously cares about the impression she makes. That is to be commended."

"All right, now will the two of you please sit down and hear me out?" I asked. John sat down, but Beth refused. She remained standing in the aisle, clutching her purse to her abdomen like a shield.

"I couldn't care less what anyone wears, but I think you should look at your attire in relationship to your life," I continued. "And this will take us right back to Beth's original question about challenge and aliveness. Society seeks to mold everyone into ladies and gentlemen wearing the mask of proper attire, manners and etiquette. Ladies and gentlemen do the right thing and say the right thing. Conventionality molds mediocrity in the form of social masks to hide the man and woman you really are beneath the disguise. So who are you beneath those formal clothes that are just like the formal clothes of a hundred thousand others in this city?"

"Masks are valuable," Beth responded. "When you let people see who you really are, you lose them."

"That's one of the dangers you face when you take off your mask," I replied. "Some people won't have anything to do with you unless you are what **they** want you to be. But if you look at that logically, it means that the relationship is based solely on your willingness to allow them to manipulate you into being what they want you to be. Unless you comply, they'll reject you. Great relationship! Do you need that?"

Neither one responded, so I continued. "I'm talking about repression ... every one of us in this room experiences repression." I turned slowly, scanning the two hundred participants filling the hotel ballroom. "Our fear-based emotions repress us. Our anger, selfishness, jealousy, hate, envy, greed, possessiveness,

16

arrogance, egotism, vanity, malice, resentment, insecurity, inhibitions and guilt. Like society, these fears mold us. And there are many other factors that mold us, generating repression.

"The expectations of others, if we accept them, mold us. And they dominate, cripple and paralyze us. The expectations of others are your enemies. You may accept some responsibilities for your mate, children and career, but aside from that, you need to look at how much of your life is ruled by the expectations of others. Expectations are the enemy of freedom."

"I lost my husband because I wasn't what he wanted me to be," Beth said loudly, starting to cry. "And I've lost friends when I haven't lived up to their expectations."

"Beth, you said you have more challenge than you know what to do with in your life, but there is no joy in it. Exactly what are the challenges you are talking about?"

"Well, just keeping up with all my responsibilities to my family and friends, and I've over-committed to volunteer work."

"Is the volunteer work a place to hide from yourself?" I asked.

"I don't know about that, but it keeps me from thinking about things that are painful. Time goes by very quickly."

"That's hiding, Beth. What about your responsibilities to family and friends?"

"Well ... it's just ... ah, well, I guess it is their expectations I'm responding to. When I think about it, they do have a lot of expectations. I don't ever seem to have any time to myself, which bothers me, but there is no one to blame."

"So you wear masks in an attempt to be everything to everyone? Will wearing masks save you from losing anyone else? You're hiding from yourself and you're hiding what you really are from everyone else. What are you, Beth?"

17

She looked at me with wide eyes for several seconds. "I don't know ... I don't know," she cried, lowering her head into her hand and sobbing. I walked over and hugged her, then whispered in her ear, "Please sit down, there is a lot more you need to hear."

Beth moved back to her seat and I returned my attention to the rest of the group. "When I talk about challenge, I'm not talking about creating busy work or places to hide. I'm talking about doing what you really enjoy doing; that which you do naturally and well, that which is fun and exciting and joyful. Challenge isn't work; it is stretching yourself to become all you are capable of being." I glanced over at John to see if he had anything to add or to ask. He made a gesture signifying that he didn't.

(**Note:** In a later process exploring cause in an altered state of consciousness, Beth discovered some forgotten programming. Following the session, she shared, "I relived an incident as a child. The only way to get my father's approval was to pretend to be a perfect little girl who accepted everything he believed in. In high school, I drew a peace sign on my notebook and my father tore it up and didn't speak to me for a week." Beth is also the subject of another dialogue later in the book.)

*There are many
easy things
that you cannot
do easily
without training.*

18

3.
Samuel

"I do not agree with you about wearing social masks," Samuel said. He was a casually dressed man in his late forties, showing no signs of hostility, but very firm in his declaration. "Masks help people to get along with each other. They make life easier for everyone."

"Repression does not make life easier for anyone, Samuel," I replied. "Masks are repression ... repressing what you really are because you don't think what you really are is acceptable. And masks always kill aliveness."

"If I didn't wear a mask as a corporate executive, I wouldn't have a job," he responded. "I have to be cordial and express high energy at all times."

"Samuel, I'm not saying to throw away all your masks, but I would advise you to find out why you wear them. The reason will always be the fear of losing someone or something. And next, I'd tell you to look into the price you pay for wearing each mask."

"Being cordial and enthusiastic isn't that big a price to pay," Samuel responded.

"The repression isn't the price, Samuel. The manifestations of repression are the price. Do you go home at night feeling negativity in the form of frustrations, stress, anxiety or anger?"

"Sure, but so does everyone else in the country," he countered.

"Wrong, Samuel. Not everyone. But it is certainly one of the primary reasons that most people's lives don't work. The negativity can manifest in any of thousands of ways. It can slowly eat away at your health, or maybe it manifests as an ulcer or skin rash. Or maybe you deal with the negativity by kicking the dog or fighting with your wife; maybe you hide from yourself with drugs or alcohol. Or maybe it manifests as an ongoing depression. Some people keep it in for years and it

19

eventually comes out as cancer."

Samuel stood looking at me without saying anything, so I asked him, "What would be the worst that would happen if you took off your masks at work and expressed who you really are?"

"As I said before, I'd probably lose my job," he responded.

"Why? Is who you are so terrible that they'd have to fire you?" I asked.

"No, but if I started being straight about the phony people and manipulating practices and scams, they'd have to fire me."

"Do you like your job, Samuel?"

"No, but I'm well paid." ‾

"Do you think you lose self-esteem remaining in this job?"

"Maybe," he replied, after a period of silence. "I've never really thought about it before. I probably do, I probably do."

"So, if you were fired tomorrow, what would happen? Would you starve to death in the gutter?" I asked.

Samuel flashed me a "don't be cute" look, stared at the floor and then at the ceiling. and eventually said, "The worst that would happen is that I'd be forced to go out and find a job I enjoy more. I might have to take a cut in pay, but I doubt it."

"So maybe the reason you're wearing your masks isn't valid anymore?" I queried.

"I don't understand," he said.

"Samuel, maybe the reason you wear your masks isn't valid because the fear behind the masks doesn't relate to your life today."

Samuel nodded his head affirmatively and sat down. And I continued with a short talk about some of the more common masks I've observed people wearing.

20

"The mask of indifference is the one where the wearer pretends it doesn't matter or pretends he doesn't care. The dumb mask is another I often see. Women tend to wear it more frequently than men. The woman pretends to be dumb, because if she didn't pretend to be dumb, she'd have to face a reality she doesn't want to face or she'd have to acknowledge facts that she'd prefer to ignore.

"I'm sure you're aware of the talker mask. This is worn by people who can't keep quiet because they are nervous or insecure about something. Often they're just nervous or insecure about allowing room in their lives for silence, because they think if they're not talking ninety miles an hour, others will feel ignored and they'll have to feel guilty for ignoring them.

"How about the funny person mask—the man or woman who constantly jokes, or throws witty remarks into every conversation? They are being funny because they need excessive attention, which is insecurity, or this is a mask to avoid an issue—anything from simple matters all the way to major confrontations. Often the person wearing this mask is deflecting real contact or intimacy.

"Now, as I'm talking about masks, I hope you are relating my words to yourself. There are thousands of masks, including the quiet mask. Some people sit back and remain quiet because they are afraid they might expose themselves by saying something stupid. Others wear the quiet mask because they feel superior.

"Even being a workaholic is a mask to avoid something. It could be to avoid undesired social contact or to avoid intimate interaction at home. Or maybe it is just a greed mask. A greed mask is generally a rationalization to work extra hours because of some financial need. But usually when I explore that one, I find the individual has created the financial need to justify the work. This can also be a martyr mask.

"The 'poor little me' mask is the favorite of problem-oriented people. A life full of problems gives the wearer something to talk about. People pretend to feel sorry for them and they get attention.

"The mask I've most often encountered is the 'extra-nice' mask. These people think they should be extra nice to everyone. It could be that these people simply get off on being needed, thus this mask is really a little power number. They get to feel superior: 'I'm always there when she needs me,' and the ego gets pumped up. Usually, though, these people are extra nice because they are afraid that other people won't like them if they are themselves. So they attempt to make everyone feel good by being extra nice. Why? Because if other people feel uncomfortable, they will feel uncomfortable, and they fear this.

"You'll also find that those who wear an extra-nice mask are usually overpowered by others in a very short time. Then they need to hide away to recuperate. Their mask gets so heavy that they have to be alone for a while to regain the strength to hold the mask up again. But if they were direct and honest in their communications, they would have no reason to hide, no reason to need to recoup their strength. The secret to throwing away all your masks is simply to be who and what you really are beneath the masks.

"Nothing about us can be changed until it is first recognized and accepted as **what is**. If you're unhappy with your life, you must recognize your masks, which is another way of saying your **patterns** in life. Your masks represent your **patterned behavior**, your habitual way of representing yourself. As you break up the patterns by taking off your masks, you get in touch with your **True Self**, and you experience aliveness. I challenge you to take off your masks."

4.
Margie

Margie was in her early twenties and very outgoing. Her sunny personality and enthusiasm had proven to be contagious to others in the seminar. "You're saying you lose your aliveness when you aren't challenged or when you allow fears to repress you? Is that right?"

"Right," I responded.

"Well, I don't disagree with that, but I'm having a hard time putting that together with spirituality. This is a spiritual seminar. Challenge isn't spiritual. I want to advance spiritually and my goal is to be part of the utopia of the New Age."

"What will that utopia be like?" I asked.

"Well ... it will be a beautiful environment of total peace and absolute tranquility," she said.

"That sounds inviting," I replied. "What would you do all day in utopia?"

"Oh, you wouldn't have to do anything but lie around and absorb the love, listen to beautiful, soothing New Age music, and just resonate and vibrate with others on your soul frequency."

"Don't you think that would get boring after a while?" I asked.

"No!" she said indignantly, scowling at me.

"Margie, no one on this planet can handle doing nothing. Maybe your ideas relate to being in spirit, without a physical body, but I doubt even that. My own understanding of the spiritual realms is that you have tasks and studies there as well as here. But the utopia you describe would include no yin-yang energy so you would automatically destroy it. The physical world is subject to the physical laws of energy. You'd have to generate some excitement, some challenge ... some aliveness. Eve would have to take a bite out of the forbidden apple or Adam would have to create rock and roll to balance the heavenly music. That's just how energy works, and as long as we're on this earth, we'll be dealing with the realities of what is."

"I don't understand what you said about the yin-yang energy," she said.

"The universe functions as a yin-yang balance, existing as a result of tension between positive and negative (yin = negative, yang = positive). All human beings contain dual aspects: love/hate, harmony/chaos, good/evil. As a natural expression of this law of opposites, that which is totally successful tends to destroy itself. I've already discussed this earlier in regard to how energy works. When you reach that pinnacle in any area of your life, you greatly increase the potential for self-destruction unless you create new challenges.

"Intuitively, you know you must express this yin-yang tension which is necessary for structure to exist," I continued. "Again, this is how energy works. You need one to have the other. To know white, you need to experience black. Positive and negative tension are necessary, as a scientific fact, for structure to exist. And human beings are structures. Without the tension between positive and negative, you couldn't exist."

"So you're saying we must express negativity to exist?" Margie asked, now scowling even more.

"Yes, I am, but let me explain it before you get even more upset with me. From a universal, spiritual perspective, there is no duality, thus no judgment. So negativity wouldn't be negative as you view it. It would just be part of the all that is. An automobile battery provides a good analogy. One plate is charged positively, the next negatively, and so on. The energy bounces from the positive to the negative and back again, interacting—charging and discharging, thus creating the energy source in your car."

"Well, that isn't really expressing negativity as I think of it then," Margie stated, without the scowl.

"Wrong, Margie. Most people express their duality quite negatively, and it's one of the reasons most people's lives don't work. You have to express both sides of your duality to keep this necessary tension in balance. Some examples of the expression of yin energy might be self-denial, such as fasting or an extreme spiritual discipline. An excess of hard work would be an expression of yin energy. So would dangerous activities, such as driving too fast or participating in dangerous sports. Gambling is a yin expression. To generate yin energy, I've seen a lot of metaphysical and religious people create threats, such as evil spirits, devils and possession. Sadly, though, arguing and fighting are the primary expressions of yin energy. Illness and war are the ultimate expressions of yin energy. So look around you. Look at your life, read the newspapers and watch the eleven o'clock news ... there is certainly ample expression of yin energy."

"This is all very depressing," Margie said, now crossing her arms. "What I'm getting from you is, no matter how spiritual we become, we'll still end up expressing yin energy, so we'll never make it. So why bother?"

"No, Margie," I responded. "I contend you can replace disharmonious expressions of yin energy with challenge ... **positive challenge**. When you do this, you retain your balance and you can easily move forward spiritually. Challenge is critical to your spiritual development."

"Wow!" Margie cried enthusiastically.

"Remember that energy must, by its very nature, move forward or backward; it must create or transform. To keep it moving forward, you need challenges. And, of course, this is where it gets touchy. If you don't incorporate challenge into your life, your subconscious will attempt to create it, and not always to your liking. But if you create too much challenge, it could also result in self-destruction. In other words, if you decide to take on the challenge of sailing a boat to Hawaii, but you don't have the necessary navigational skills, you'll probably be lost at sea. The goal is to keep challenge in balance. You must consciously direct challenge in a way that minimizes jeopardy while still fulfilling the yin-yang balance. This is usually accomplished by **wise risking**. No matter how successful you are, always give yourself new and greater challenges in all areas of your life: your relationships, career, spirituality, hobbies, and even service to others and to the planet."

> *To become a*
> *Master of Life*
> *is to abandon*
> *all self-deception,*
> *all myths,*
> *all cosmic daydreams,*
> *all beguiling fairy stories*
> *which keep you from*
> *understanding the*
> *true nature of your life.*

5.
Susan

Susan raised her hand to share, then stood up and started talking before I recognized her. She was in her early thirties, conservatively dressed. "You talk about letting negativity flow through you without affecting you, but I'd challenge anyone to do this with my mother-in-law. She is deliberately hateful. She must sit up nights thinking of ways to cause us trouble."

"Okay, Susan, let's begin at the beginning. Tell me how you mentally deal with your mother-in-law. Do you think about her often, and do you talk about her with your husband and friends?"

"Of course I talk about her," she responded. "That's the only thing that releases my anxiety on the subject. When I tell other people about her tricks and numbers, they can't believe it. Of course, I think about it all the time. This woman is a nut case and she makes my life miserable."

"No, she doesn't, Susan," I said. "You are making your life miserable. Obviously, your soap opera is your mother-in-law. Your challenge is also probably coming from your mother-in-law. She generates the excitement you probably don't get anywhere else."

"That's bullshit!" Susan screamed at me. "I don't need that kind of excitement in my life."

"Maybe you don't think so consciously, but you have no idea what is going on subconsciously. But let's not get stuck on that. Let's take a moment and explore how the mind works. Your mind works like a computer. Every thought programs that computer. The data processing term 'GIGO'—garbage in, garbage out— is very appropriate. In other words, if you program your subconscious mind, your computer, with negative garbage, you'll have to experience future negativity as a result. This is simply cause and effect, which is karma.

"Every time you repeat your soap opera about your mother-in-law to other people, you program a little more negativity ... and a little more negativity. Thoughts are things and they create karma, so every time you think negative thoughts about your mother-in-law, you program a little more negativity. This negativity has to come out, Susan. It has to generate other negative experiences or negative health. So what I am saying to you is that you are making your life even more miserable by reacting the way you are reacting to your mother-in-law. It sounds like it's already bad enough. Why make it worse?"

"But if I didn't talk about it, I'd go crazy. My talking releases the frustrated energy," she explained.

"You think it does," I told her. "And as long as you feel the frustrations, you'll probably talk about it. One of the reasons you feel better is that those close to you sympathize with you and you get to feel like a poor little victim. You get attention, and everyone needs attention. It makes you feel good."

"Oh, to hell with you," Susan responded. "I'm not looking for attention! I'm looking for relief."

"Don't take this personally, Susan, but with few exceptions **everything** you and everyone else says is to attain sympathy or make themselves seem more important."

"That's ridiculous!"

"No, it isn't. Over the course of a few weeks, you might relate a few facts and figures and accomplish some work, but your verbal communications are always oriented to make you appear just a bit more important in the eyes of others, or as an attempt to get sympathy. Once you start observing and listening to yourself, you'll get it. But let's get back to the point. Can you truthfully tell me that you don't have a lot of additional negativity in your life? Negativity other than with your mother-in-law?"

"Well, I guess so," she admitted, thinking about it. "My husband and I fight a lot, and not just about his mother. But mostly it's just little screw-ups, accidents or stresses that make life more difficult than I'd like it to be."

"What about your physical health?"

"Well, I get stomachaches a lot, but I asked the doctor about it and I don't have ulcers."

"Okay, Susan," I continued. "I think it would be accurate to assume some of the additional negativity, and maybe even your stomach problems, relate to self-

28

programmed negativity. So now let's look at the real problem, which is your reaction to your mother-in-law. Your mother-in-law is conniving and manipulating, is that what is?"

"It certainly is," Susan smiled.

"Okay, so that's what is. That may not be the way you want it to be, but what is, is, and there is nothing you can do about it but send her light and love. Now, why do you suppose she does what she does?"

Susan thought about it for several seconds and said, "It's how she gets her kicks. I have no doubt that she enjoys making people react to her. Maybe it's just the game she plays to make life more interesting for her, to get her aliveness, as you call it."

"Of course it's her game, Susan. And you also choose to play her game the moment you start resisting her. It is your resistance that causes your pain. And it is a Universal Law: That which you resist, you draw to yourself. If you stopped resisting and simply refused to play—refused to react and resist—there would be no problem. You wouldn't be experiencing the direct frustrations, much less the programmed future negativity."

"I don't buy that," Susan responded. "That would be submitting to her."

"No, it wouldn't, Susan. It would be transcending your self-destructive game. The conscious detachment approach would be to let it go because logically you can only lose. If you could look at the situation with this enlightened viewpoint, you could let your mother-in-law's negativity flow through you without affecting you."

"Easier to say than to do," she responded.

"Conscious detachment begins with awareness. First, be aware that playing the game hurts you now and in the future; second, realize that you choose to react. I

29

have a collie who devotes her life to getting our horses to react to her efforts for attention. She barks and runs back and forth, jumping at them. One horse reacts, kicking and bucking all over the corral; the other just ignores the dog."

"Okay, I get it," Susan said. "But I keep hoping she'll change."

"You know what your mother-in-law is and you know you can't change her. To expect her to someday become reasonable, kind and loving just isn't realistic—your expectations conflict with what is."

"I should just stop playing the game," Susan said, thoughtfully.

"It would allow you to win, wouldn't it? Until now, you've been attempting to get to be right with your mother-in-law but you keep losing the game. The moment you stop playing, you win. I'm sure your mother-in-law will become very frustrated; she'll have to find someone else to play with."

"Oh, that would be awful," Susan laughed.

"And then you'll need to find new areas of aliveness," I told her. "What can you do to create positive challenge in your life?"

"I'll think of something," she promised, sitting down.

I'm not going to tell you anything you don't know. The problem is, you don't know you know.

30

6.
William & Ellen

"You advocate an approach to spirituality that goes against the teachings of almost every other New Age guru," William said quietly. "I'm afraid I have a hard time with that. Peace and balance can be found in many organized religions."

"Organized religions only offer dogma and beliefs that may or may not be based upon reality," I said. "A belief is a prejudice without real evidence to support it; you accept it on faith but you don't know. You may think you know; you might even be willing to stake your life on the fact that you know ... but you **don't** know. And religions are restrictive and self-serving, based on a dim hope in the future while robbing their followers of enjoyment in the present."

"What about all the gurus who tell you to find balance through meditation?" William responded.

"I have nothing against short meditations or self-hypnosis sessions. They are an ideal support program to assist you to create your own reality."

"No, no," he said. "I meditate for an hour each morning and each evening, and I'm much more peaceful because of it." William's wife Ellen, sitting beside him, nodded in agreement.

"Gurus and cults offer you the wisdom of Eastern thinking but they insist on combining it with lengthy meditation, mantra chanting or twirling," I said. "Excessive use of any of these techniques eventually causes your mind to go 'flat.' You may experience detachment and peace of mind, but it is artificial—a drugless tranquilizer easily explained by neurological studies. Your brain releases beta-endorphins—opium-like neurotransmitters—and you become very mellow and detached. The problem is that you detach from everything ... from the warmth and joy as well as the

31

anger and negativity. This is why these techniques are so widely used by cults to effectively control their followers."

"How much is too much?" Ellen asked, now standing beside her husband.

"That varies with the individual, but for most people to meditate, chant mantras or twirl for 40 minutes twice a day will soon keep their brains in an alpha level. I'm not saying this is bad; it might be salvation for some people. But even eyes-open alpha is the level of meditation or hypnosis, and you become very mellow and will tend to detach from those you love as well as from disharmony in your life."

"That's true," Ellen said, looking at William. "You don't have as much to say to me since you started meditating. Me or anyone else. You are certainly mellow, but I'd like to see some of your old fire again."

William didn't respond, so I continued. "When I was in a disharmonious relationship, I used to run several miles a day. Once conditioned, your body starts releasing beta-endorphins around the one mile point of the run. Running was great for my aerobics. It allowed me to detach from the disharmonious relationship and handle it because I was 'stoned' on beta-endorphins. The same thing happens when you meditate to excess. Anyway, that relationship ended in a divorce. Later, when I established a harmonious relationship with my wife, Tara, I found I was running less and less. I didn't need the detachment. I still believe in the value of running but I keep my miles down to a point where I remain in beta."

"But you yourself said one needs to detach to attain enlightenment," William objected.

"Right, William, but I teach **conscious detachment**. It is based upon logic and is workable in contemporary society. The test of any teaching or technique is, does it help you? If it doesn't help you, what good is it? A true

32

teaching must assist you to become more natural, and it must be workable in your own world. If the teachings are so 'airy-fairy' that they don't relate to reality, or if they are only valuable in the protected environment of a cult where you wear purple robes, I think you're wasting your time. If you want to achieve enlightenment, end suffering and attain peace of mind, you don't need psychiatrists, psychologists, religions, priests, evangelists or gurus. There is no one to save you but yourself."

7.
Linda

"Obviously, what you are saying about energy, challenge and aliveness is logical, which is more than I can say for most spiritual communications, but what about the goal? I know you accept reincarnation and karma because of the many books you've written on the subject, but why are we here, now, living on this planet?" Linda was probably in her mid-thirties, attractive, casually dressed and at ease speaking in front of the group.

"I can only share my truth, Linda, and that is, you are here because you want to evolve spiritually, and this is a process of letting go of fear and learning to express unconditional love. You have karma and dharma to fulfill, but they're only the rules you've chosen to play the game. The game has always been to let go of fear and express unconditional love."

"How can you expect me to love everyone on this planet unconditionally when I've never even seen two people capable of loving each other unconditionally?" Linda asked.

"That's a pretty good argument," I replied. "But just because we aren't surrounded with living examples doesn't mean it isn't possible. Don't you think Jesus, Buddha and Krishna loved unconditionally? Of course they did; all Masters love unconditionally. Our spiritual quest will someday lead us to become a Master."

"I think we're all a long way from becoming Masters," Linda laughed.

"Maybe," I said, "but you asked why we are here. Supreme enlightenment would be to become a Master. Jesus himself told us this in the Bible when he responded to his disciples, who were awed by the miracles he performed. Jesus turned to them and said, 'These things ye too shall do and more.' We will all be Masters someday, capable of literally creating our own reality."

"So, you're saying that someday, many lifetimes from now, we will finally be capable of loving unconditionally?" Linda asked.

"No, I'm saying you can start right now," I replied. "As we begin to let go of fear, we automatically become capable of expressing unconditional love. Actually, I'm talking about one thing, not two. As you purposely express unconditional love, you let go of fear and vice versa. When you accept others as they are, without attempting to change them, without blame or judgment, you express unconditional love."

"Okay, you're not talking about love-type love, are you?" Linda asked.

"Romantic human love? No, I'm not. But if unconditional love were combined with romantic love, you would have the ultimate love—twin flame, soulmate love. First, let's look at how a Master loves unconditionally. He would not love as we think of love, for a Master is love. Human love is found in the way you feel and behave to create a relationship between yourself and another. But a Master's love is an essence, a totality. Think of a Master as a flower in a garden. As you pass, you inhale the fragrance of the flower. The flower didn't send the fragrance to you specifically; it was there when no one was there to enjoy it. And if no

34

one ever passed by, the fragrance would still be there.

"Obviously, most of us won't evolve to the level of a Master in one lifetime," I continued. "But if this is our goal, now is the time to begin. I contend that you can advance many lifetimes in the time you have left in this life, if you make the conscious decision to do so. Ancient Zen teaching offers the **Three Principal Aspects of the Path to Supreme Enlightenment**. First is **the determination to be free of the cyclical existence of reincarnation,** meaning that you make a conscious decision to live in a way that generates only harmonious or neutral karma. Second is **the correct view of emptiness.** I teach this as conscious detachment. Third is **to develop an altruistic mind of enlightenment,** which I teach as the expression of unconditional love.

"These three steps eventually lead to the level of Master. And I believe they can be further simplified to the concept of learning to let go of fear and learning to express unconditional love."

"Does your idea of unconditional love include loving everyone as yourself?" Linda asked, thinking very deeply about my words.

"Let me answer that by first sharing the four assumptions that underlie all Eastern philosophy and metaphysical awareness," I replied. "First is the concept that **all is one**. The external world and consciousness are one and the same. **Second** is the idea that **man is a Divine being**. We are all part of God, so we are God. Third is the thought that **life is for evolutionary purposes**. Reincarnation and karma offer the path to spiritual evolution. Fourth is **self-actualization**: awareness of the True Self within leads to enlightenment.

"All right, I'd like to explore the first and second assumptions. How can we all be one? And how is the external and consciousness the same thing? As we spiritually evolve and become capable of expressing more and more unconditional love, we move deeper and deeper into our own **center**. At this point, deep within our unconscious mind, is the **collective unconscious**. And at this level, we are all one. All souls, living and in spirit, are connected. The collective unconscious is the God level; it is from this level that all great insights emerge. We just have to look within to discover that we are God. The way to experience this awareness is to learn to express unconditional love in everything we think, say and do.

"Unconditional love transcends everything else. It is the only tangible thing in life; everything else is illusion. We don't need Ten Commandments, or Buddha's Eight-Fold Plan; we don't need preachers or philosophers or gurus. All we need is the awareness to express unconditional love in response to every situation we encounter."

"If you can accept this idea, you are far more enlightened than most people on this planet. As a whole, people need ritual and dogma. We are conditioned to believe that answers are hidden, known only to those who have spent their lives studying, or who are somehow 'special' enough to succeed in channeling wisdom from the spiritual realms. Well, guess what? That's not what is."

*Never do anything
that you'll have
to punish
yourself for.*

Section Two
How To End Suffering And Attain Peace of Mind

If you want to end suffering and attain peace of mind, your only help is **self-help**! Unless you need hospital treatment or prescription drugs, all that gurus, religions or mental health counselors can do to help you is: 1. alter your viewpoint, or 2. make you aware of your unconscious programming. **The rest is up to you.**

This section offers awareness that will assist you to fully comprehend the dialogues that follow. Four concepts are given that will allow you to end suffering and attain peace of mind. That may sound presumptuous, but that's what is. The concepts are the answer. It's quite simple, but that doesn't mean it's easy. It takes time to become fully aware of the wisdom which can erase your disharmonious karma. It also takes time and self-discipline to incorporate this awareness into your life. But when you do, it will serve as the foundation from which you'll express unconditional love.

To be a **Master of Life** in today's society means to be self-actualized and aware in a very unaware world that wants you to fit its mold and accept its ideas. These teachings offer a philosophy/religion of self that you don't join ... you live. The awareness is the soul of spirituality and is based upon Zen, metaphysics, logic, contemporary therapy and brain/mind research.

1.
Karma & Reincarnation

Accept karma as your philosophical basis of reality. In so doing, you accept total self-responsibility.

Reincarnation was taught by Buddha, Krishna and Rama, and is part of all the great Eastern religions. It is also taught by contemporary metaphysical organizations, and as you are probably already aware, these great teachers, religions and groups don't agree on much except the concept of reincarnation. Reincarnation was taught by the Essenes, with whom Jesus had considerable contact. The historian Josephus refers to reincarnation as a common belief among Jews at the time of Jesus.

Several references to reincarnation appear to remain in the Christian Bible although most were deleted. Some of the Old Testament books were compiled no earlier than the seventh and eighth centuries B.C. Jesus' teachings were not written down in his lifetime but were handed down verbally from disciple to disciple. Most of the New Testament was written in the second and third centuries A.D.

In tracing the origin of the Bible, one is led to A.D. 325, when Constantine the Great called the First Council of Nicaea, composed of 300 religious leaders. Three centuries after Jesus lived, this council was given the task of separating divinely inspired writings from those of questionable origin.

The actual compilation of the Bible was an incredibly complicated project that involved churchmen of many

38

varying beliefs, in an atmosphere of dissension, jealousy, intolerance, persecution and bigotry.

At this time, the question of the divinity of Jesus had split the church into two factions. Constantine offered to make the little-known Christian sect the official state religion if the Christians would settle their differences. Apparently, he didn't particularly care what they believed in as long as they agreed upon a belief. By compiling a book of sacred writings, Contantine thought that the book would give authority to the new church. It is a matter of historical record that only after much hostility and bitterness at the Council of Nicaea was Jesus declared to be the "Essence of the Father."

The fact that reincarnation had at one time been in the Bible is indisputable, for in A.D. 533, during the Second Council of Constantinople, the church adopted a decree stating:

> Whosoever shall support the mythical doctrine of the pre-existence of the soul and the subsequent wonderful opinion of its return, let him be anathema.

Nothing can be canceled by official decree unless its existence is being acknowledged in the first place! Reincarnation was probably removed because the church leaders thought it let people be independent by allowing them self-responsibility for their own actions and the opportunity to balance karma in future lives. These leaders decided it was better to tell people, "There is only one life. If you don't live the way we tell you is the right way to live, you'll go to hell." That made it much easier to control the masses.

So, if you accept that reincarnation was once also part of Christianity, then it becomes the core belief of almost all spirituality in the world. And the system that makes reincarnation workable and logical is **karma**.

It is easy to say you accept karma, but I've found that most people do not fully comprehend what that means.

It is easy to explain karma in one sentence: If you act positively, you'll experience harmony, and if you act negatively, you'll experience disharmony. The word karma means action. And there are three kinds of action:

1. Mental action
2. Verbal action
3. Physical action

From a karmic viewpoint, the effect of your actions are harmonious, disharmonious or neutral. Karma is personal and collective. The world we are currently experiencing has been formed by our collective karma.

If you want to know about your past karma, simply look at your current state of mind, your body, your success or lack of success, your relationships ... or lack of them. If you want to know what will happen in the future, look at what your mind concentrates on now. On a regular basis, what do you think about? Pettiness, gossip, small talk, negativity? Or do you dwell upon positive things, loving emotions, compassion and service?

You are creating your own future right now, and you can view this from the perspective of cause and effect in the context of your present life. Everything you've ever experienced is recorded in the memory banks of your subconscious mind. According to brain researchers, your subconscious mind has 200,000 times the capacity of the largest computer ever built, so recording your entire past isn't too great a task. These past experiences represent all your programming and it is your programming that has made you what you are today. Your talents and abilities, problems and afflictions are the result of your past programming, which is your karma.

You create your own reality, or karma, as a response to everything you **think, say** and **do**. But to begin with, you must understand that **karma either is or it isn't**. It is

40

not a halfway proposition. This is either a random universe or there is meaning to life.

The nihilistic viewpoint is that we came from nowhere—we just appeared—and when we die, we become nothing ... no reason, no plan, no point to our existence. Life is totally meaningless. Or there is a plan behind existence. If there is a plan, then an intelligence must be behind the plan. You can call the intelligence by any name you desire: God, universal mind, energy gestalt, collective unconscious, to name a few.

And if there is a plan, it follows that justice must be part of it. Justice! But look around you. Where is there justification for misery and inequality? How can you justify child abuse, mass starvation, rapes, murders, wars, victims of violence, people ripping off other people and seemingly being rewarded for it?

Karma can explain it all! I've studied philosophy and religion all my life and nothing else can logically explain the inequality. Karma rewards and punishes. It is a multi-life debit and credit system that offers total justice. But what we can't forget is that karma either is or it isn't. There can be no halfway plan, no halfway justice. Either absolutely everything is karmic or nothing is karmic. You need to accept or reject the concept of karma; it is senseless and confusing to accept a halfway position.

Now, to bring some of this awareness together: If I pick up a stone and toss it into a pond, I am the cause and the effect is the splash and ripples. I have disturbed the harmony of the pond. The ripples flow out and back until, due to the physical law of dissipation of energy, the pond eventually returns to its original harmonious state.

And, like the rock, everything negative that you think, say or do creates vibrations that flow out and back until eventually, through your lifetimes, you balance your karma ... until your own harmony is

41

restored. Everything you **think**, **say** and **do** creates or erases karma. And, if that were not enough to deal with, this includes the **motive, intent** and **desire** behind every thought and action.

When you begin to explore the motive, intent and desire behind everything you think, say and do, you'll find you're asking yourself a lot of questions. Are you helping your friend out of true compassion or because it pumps up your ego? Or because your friend is now in debt to you? Do you give to charity at the office because you desire to help, or because you are afraid of what people in the office will think if you don't? It's easy to appear to be creating harmonious karma when you really aren't, because of your motive, intent or desire. **Why** you do what you do is just as important as **what** you do from a karmic perspective.

I also contend that neither God nor the Lords of Karma bestow your suffering upon you. It is **your** decision and **yours alone** to tackle the opportunities you are experiencing in your life. Only you are responsible for absolutely everything that has ever happened to you. You are your own judge and jury. In your Higher Mind, you are fully aware that in order to progress, you must learn. And the fastest way to learn is by directly experiencing the actual consequences of your own actions.

And, if you and you alone are responsible for absolutely everything that has ever happened to you, that means **everything**! That means (and this is very hard for some people to accept) there is no one to blame for **anything** that has ever happened to you. **There is no one to blame for anything!** The concept of blame is totally incompatible with karma. There are no victims. The ex-mate you had such a hard time with, the partner who ripped you off, the in-laws you hated, your sadistic boss, the guy who raped you when you were only 12, the burglars who robbed your house ... you created them all because you needed the self-punishment **or** you wanted to test yourself.

Take a moment and think back on your life. Think about everyone in your past who really made life difficult for you. In actuality, these were the people who helped you the most in accomplishing your goal of spiritual evolution. They helped you balance your karma. They were a test you created to determine how well you're progressing in attaining a perspective of Unconditional Love.

It is easy to tell whether you are passing or failing your own tests. If you respond with love, positive thoughts and compassion, you are probably passing the test. If you respond with negativity and blame, you are probably failing. And if you choose to fail, that is all right ... you'll just have to come back and try it again! If neither one learns this time, you will come back together in a future life for another opportunity. If one learns and the other doesn't, the one who learns has resolved the karma. The one who didn't will find someone else with a similar karmic configuration and they will come together to test themselves in the future.

Often in balancing karma you don't even have to wait for the next lifetime for an opportunity to arise. We have all observed recurring, undesirable patterns in others, as well as ourselves. This is a situation of learning through **pain** until we finally "get it," once and for all, that what we are doing doesn't work.

You were born with the package of karma that you desired to experience. From a spiritual perspective, if you are testing yourself, it is only your reactions to the experiences that are important.

When we are on the other side in spirit, preparing to enter into a lifetime, I sometimes think we go through a period of what I call being "very brave."

For instance, you may say to yourself, "Okay, I think I'm ready to test myself in another relationship with

Donald. If he's willing, we'll fall in love, get married and have three children. When I'm about 32, Donald will begin to ignore me and start having affairs with other women. This time, because I owe Don one in this area, I'll emotionally support him and let him go with unconditional love."

As I said, you are "very brave" and aware over there on the other side. Now comes the reality. And what do you do? You scream and threaten and blame. You hire a lawyer who socks it to Donald financially for the rest of his days. You and Donald now hate each other. This is another example of learning through pain. You and Don can plan to return for another round in the year 2046; maybe the next time you will work it out.

Actually, there is no such thing as failing your own karmic test. If you fell off your bicycle nine times before you finally learned to ride, the nine failures were actually small successes which eventually led to the ultimate success. How many times you fail before reaching your goal is up to you.

In addition to your birth karma, you are creating new karma every day, both harmonious and disharmonious. And you are paying it off every day through the balancing effects of your subconscious mind.

There is also karma as yet unknown to you. It is stored up from the past, waiting for a suitable opportunity to discharge itself. This could happen later in this life or in your next life or in a lifetime after that. Not everything can be balanced in one lifetime.

But the good news is the Law of Grace supersedes the Law of Karma. This means that if you give love, grace and mercy, you will receive it in return. All of your positive and loving thoughts and actions go to cancel your stored-up, bad karma. And since this is so, it is probably time for you to begin to think about how you can be more positive, loving and compassionate; how you can support good works and serve this planet ... if only to reduce the amount of undesirable karma that you have waiting for you in your future.

I also contend that **wisdom erases karma** and that we can mitigate karmic discomforts through awareness. The techniques of past-life therapy are often of value in this area. In the past, we've learned through pain. In other words, we've learned not to touch hot stoves because by touching hot stoves, we burn our fingers. After experiencing the pain of touching many hot stoves, we finally learn, once and for all, that it doesn't work to touch hot stoves. Of course, the hot stoves are the karmic lessons we need to learn in the areas of physical life, relationships, respect for life, greed, etc.

Instead, by learning through wisdom, we accept what we need to learn by becoming aware of the lesson, forgiving ourselves and letting go of it. Karma simply seeks to restore your disturbed equilibrium. You can do it the hard way through pain ... or the easy way through wisdom and grace.

Of course, to learn through wisdom, you must **forgive yourself**. Since you are your own judge and jury, it is up to you to forgive yourself. The only problem is that you will not do this unless you feel that the karma is totally balanced or that the lesson is learned. You can't fool yourself in this area. To truly forgive yourself, you must know, on every level of your body and mind, that you will never, ever forget the lesson again.

If you are not yet able to forgive yourself to this degree, you must decide what you can do to achieve this desired level of self-forgiveness. Can you do something symbolic to show that you have learned? Can you assist others as a form of restitution?

In working with people in past-life therapy, I've found that what I call "symbolic restitution" can be very powerful. As an example, I'll share the case of a man who suffered severe back problems for most of his adult

45

life. Medically, nothing was found to be wrong with him. In regression, he relived a past life as a soldier in World War I. During battle, an artillery shell exploded near him, sending shrapnel into his back. He died slowly, in great pain, over a period of several days, feeling much bitterness toward the enemy.

With this knowledge revealed, he decided to become actively involved in the peace movement. This was a couple of years ago, and since then, he has strongly supported world peace organizations. And his back is slowly improving.

In another case, a woman with a long history of relationship problems relived a past life as a man who mistreated, raped and beat many women. As a form of symbolic restitution, the woman began volunteering her time to assist in a clinic for battered women. In this way, she will quickly attain, through wisdom, an awareness of the pain caused by such actions.

Self-Testing Karma

All karma can be categorized as self-reward or self-punishment. And, from a larger perspective, all karma is self-testing. This simply means that you create a situation to test yourself to see if you have learned your lessons on every level of your body and mind.

Self-testing could easily be combined with reward karma. Suppose you have earned the karmic right to easy wealth and fame. It is also a very important self-test to see if you can handle it correctly from a karmic perspective. Do you use the money and position selfishly or do you use it as an opportunity to assist others? Often, the results of the test will indicate if you will allow yourself to retain the reward throughout your entire lifetime.

Another reward example might be a good marriage. Your test comes when the marriage hits a bumpy road.

How do the two of you handle it? Let's say that you both respond with love. Chances are you'll remain together and not have to experience the more intense and long-range pain that would have resulted from the parting if you both hadn't learned your karmic lesson.

But let's explore it from another perspective. Let's assume that you are the female and you handle the problems with little or no compassion. You immediately leave your husband and take up with someone new. You have probably failed your own test. Now, let's say that the husband is very hurt, but he handles the parting with love and compassion and lets you go in a very supportive way. He may very well have passed his test, at the same time paying off old karma by being left. Maybe he left someone under similar circumstances in his last lifetime and he is balancing the situation.

The outcome wasn't predestined. You were both always capable of exercising your free will. Had you remained together, he may have had to wait until some future lifetime or event to balance the old debt. But since circumstances worked out the way they did, he resolved a karmic test and also karmic self-punishment in this one situation.

Self-Reward Karma

Reward karma is all the good stuff you've earned in the past. It could manifest in major aspects of life, such as easily attained wealth, a naturally healthy body or a good relationship with your mate. Or, reward karma could simply be viewed as the right to be born under more ideal astrological influences. We are all walking examples of our astrological birth times. While one set of planetary combinations may generate a mellow, self-confident personality, another combination may result in a hyperactive or self-destructive personality. Although all planetary configurations have both positive and negative aspects, some are more easily overcome than others.

Self-Punishment Karma

Self-punishment is exactly what it sounds like. You've done something disharmonious in the past and the quickest way to learn is to directly experience the consequences of your actions.

As an example, let's say you find yourself in a situation of extreme poverty to balance a past life in which you totally misused wealth. This is self-punishment. It is also self-testing, for your life is so miserable that it would be easy to turn to crime or to commit suicide. The test is to live through it properly.

The Five Categories of Karma

There are five categories of karma which fall either under self-reward or self-punishment.

Balancing Karma

This is the most simplistic, mechanical kind of cause and effect. Examples of balancing karma would be a lonely man who seeks unsuccessfully to establish a relationship. In a past life, he used others so cruelly that he needs to learn the value of a relationship.

Other examples: a man who is always overlooked for promotion because in a past life he destroyed others to attain wealth and power; a woman who suffers continual, severe migraine headaches because, in a fit of jealousy, she hit her lover on the head and killed him in a past incarnation; a man who is born blind because as a Roman soldier he purposely blinded Christian prisoners.

Physical Karma

Physical karma is a situation in which a past-life problem or misuse of the body results in an appropriate

48

affliction in a later life.

As an example, a child born with lung problems might relate back to excessive smoking and death from lung cancer in a past life. Another man with a large, disfiguring birthmark found that it was a carry-over from a terrible burn in a past incarnation.

False-Fear Karma

False-fear karma is created when a traumatic past-life incident generates a fear that is not valid in the context of the current life.

For example, a workaholic finds out in regression that he couldn't feed his family during a time of famine in the Middle Ages. He re-experiences the pain of burying a child who starved to death. In his current life, his subconscious mind is attempting to avert any potential duplication of that terrible mental pain, thus generating an internal drive to work day and night and assure that he adequately provides for his family in this incarnation.

False-fear karma and guilt karma are the easiest to resolve through past-life therapy techniques because once the individuals understand the origin of the fear and/or guilt, they can see how it no longer applies to them in their current lifetime.

False-Guilt Karma

False-guilt karma occurs when an individual takes on the responsibility or accepts the blame for a traumatic past-life incident for which he or she is blameless from any perspective.

A man who contracted polio resulting in a paralyzed leg perceived as the past-life cause his being the driver of a car which was involved in an accident that crippled a child. Although it wasn't his fault, he blames himself and seeks self-forgiveness through this karmic affliction.

In another situation, a young woman with terrible physical and emotional problems regressed to a past-life in which a violent and unstable soldier was attracted to her. She was repulsed by him and did not respond to his courting. As a warning to her, if she continued to refuse him, he cut off the hands of her best friend. The woman felt responsibility and guilt over the loss of her friend's hands and, in an attempt to pay a debt she didn't owe, she created a traumatic life for herself.

Situations involving depression and/or emotional problems combined with physical problems can almost always be traced to a tragedy of some kind in which **guilt** is associated with the event. This can be false guilt or a situation in which the troubled individual was actually responsible for the tragedy.

Developed Ability and Awareness Karma

Abilities and awareness are developed over a period of many lifetimes.

A man in Rome became interested in music and began to develop his ability. Today, after six additional lifetimes in which he became a little better with each life, he is a successful professional musician.

As another example, a woman who has been happily married for 35 years has worked hard to refine her awareness of human relationships over many lifetimes.

The abilities and awareness that you master over a period of lifetimes are yours to keep forever, although they may lie latent, buried deep within you, waiting for a time when it seems appropriate to call them into your present existence.

Destiny versus Free Will

In becoming aware of karma, some people begin to feel helpless, as if everything were predestined. This is not how it works. Some things are destined when you come into a life. These are usually major life areas, and you are born with astrological configurations that dictate how you are going to approach your life opportunities. But, as you live your life, moving toward the predestined events, you can mitigate circumstances and exercise free will in your response to everything you experience. It may even be possible to live your life in such a way as to cancel the need for learning in a particular area. Wisdom eases karma and in changing how you think, act and react, you change your future.

2.
What Is, Is

What's hot is hot and what's cold is cold

The second step to assist you to end suffering and attain peace of mind is to accept that what is, is. As simple as this concept is, I've been studying it for years and I still continue to learn more about it. Life on earth includes suffering. That's pretty obvious. We have relationship problems, we lose loved ones through separation or death, we experience loneliness, sickness and accidents. We are haunted by guilt. We have monetary hardships, experience phobias and fears and have unfulfilled desires.

We experience this distress because we desire things to be different than they are. In short, it is your resistance to what is that causes your suffering. And when I say suffering, I mean everything in your life that doesn't work. Do you want to see an immediate, positive change in your life? Then stop resisting what is. Some things are facts. Income taxes exist ... that's what is. Gravity exists ... that's what is. Your mate is quiet and stubborn ... that's what is. You can spend your life attempting to change what is, but there isn't much you're going to do about it. Instead, concentrate your efforts upon that which you can change.

A short Christian prayer says the same thing: "God grant me the serenity to accept the things I cannot change, the courage to change the things I can, and the wisdom to know the difference."

But you should hear the resistance to this concept that I receive in seminars. People want things changed. In fact, they want everything they dislike changed, and initially, they think I am advocating total, passive acceptance of life as it is. That is not the case.

Maybe the powers that be have decided to build a maximum security prison a few blocks from your house. That is not necessarily what is. You have the power to gather your neighbors and petition the state to build it elsewhere. There are things you have the potential to change, so do everything you can to change them if it is important to you. But there are also things you cannot change and I advocate that you recognize these areas of your life and stop wasting your efforts attempting to change what cannot be changed.

When you begin to accept what is in your life, you simply accept facts, logic ... unalterable realities. Actually, you have no choice in accepting what is. It is what is. But you certainly have a choice in how you respond to what is. You can handle it or make it worse by generating negative subconscious programming.

The wisdom of many of the old Zen Masters have been translated and are available to be studied today. My favorite Zen Master was Joshu, and Zen expressed through Joshu is radical, extreme and sometimes even brutal. He was born in China in A.D. 778 and is believed to have died in A.D. 897 at the age of 120. My favorite Joshu story relates to his death. His students gathered around their dying master, and one asked, "Oh, Master, don't leave us without telling us the meaning of life." In response to this request, Joshu said, "What's hot is hot and what's cold is cold!" And he died. It was his way of saying, what is, is.

3.
Conscious Detachment

There is **attached** mind and **detached** mind. The vast majority of people on this planet live out their lives knowing only attached mind. This means your state of mind is always changing from positive to negative as outside conditions change. This is extreme fluctuation from happiness and joy through **neutral** to the basement of emotions: depression, anger, hostility and other fears.

Here are some examples of attached mind: 1. You are having a great day at the office until a co-worker makes a snide remark about your hair. Your response is inner anger and you dwell upon the situation for the rest of the day. 2. You climbed into the shower with your brand-new electronic watch on. The water ruins it and you become depressed. 3. You give a presentation at your club and it is well received. But afterward, someone whose opinion you respect criticizes your presentation and you respond with hostility.

The goal is to develop **detached** mind. This means your state of mind fluctuates only from positive to neutral as outside conditions change. You accept all the warmth and joy and happiness that life has to offer while detaching from negativity by allowing it to flow through you without affecting you. In other words, your state of mind drops no further than neutral.

Here are some examples of detached mind: 1. You are having a great day at the office. When a co-worker makes a snide remark about your hair, your response is to let the remark flow through you without affecting you. You know the remark says a lot more about her than it does about your hair. 2. You climb into the shower with your brand-new electronic watch on and the water ruins it. In understanding that you can do nothing about it, you accept what is. You refuse to get upset and make matters worse by programming your subconscious mind with negativity. 3. You give a presentation at your club and it is well received by all but one person, whose opinion you respect. When he criticizes your presentation, you respond, "Thank you for your opinion; that's what you got out of it." You are unaffected by the remark. You know your critic is speaking from his viewpoint which has nothing to do with the facts. You know your talk was well received and you've detached from the need to be right.

To develop conscious detachment means to detach only from the negativity in your life. It does not mean having no feelings or sensations such as hunger or pain. It is not artificial detachment based upon alpha level programming. It is detachment based upon conscious awareness of the logic of letting go and refusing to make matters worse than they already are.

I am not talking about psychological dissociation, which is a defense mechanism to avoid reality. I am not talking about repressing your natural negative emotions. As long as you feel the anger, hostility and resentment, you'll have to express it, or it will come out in another way.

But as you consciously come to realize when you are resisting what is and when you are making matters worse, you will start to back off due to **wisdom**, not repression. Be totally involved in your life and enjoy everything there is to enjoy while detaching from the negativity. When you eliminate the negativity, you leave more time and room for love and warm interaction. When you cease to be concerned about negativity, you'll be more likely to enter into what you do in life with nothing held back—free to be entirely at one with circumstance.

Until you can go through a lifetime of total involvement without generating disharmonious karma, you'll be tied to the "cyclical existence of reincarnation."

Another way to phrase that would be to say, until you can go through a lifetime of total involvement, only expressing unconditional love, you'll be tied to the cyclical existence of reincarnation. This is simply the bottom line on spiritual evolution.

4.
Viewpoint

Reality exists as that which you experience and the way you experience life is based solely upon the way you choose to view what happens to you. Your viewpoint is the deciding factor in whether you perceive life as a hostile experience or a tranquil oneness.

What you would call a negative situation in your life is only a problem if you look upon it as a problem. We all have the ability to transform the way we experience our life, or in other words, change our perspective. As difficult as it may be to accept, our problems actually contribute satisfaction to our lives. If there were no problems to challenge you, there could be no growth. There would be no way for you to learn how to handle things and become aware of your capability for making your life work.

In fact, if you didn't have problems, you'd have to invent some to give yourself the opportunity to grow and learn and make your life work. And obviously, that is often what we do. We manifest problems, not consciously, but subconsciously we create these challenges.

The real secret to growth through problems is to look upon problems as opportunities. The bigger the problem, the bigger the opportunity. And the problem usually stays with us just as long as we need it to achieve an understanding of ourselves and others. Once we have that understanding, we can let go of the effect.

In many problem situations, nothing about the situation will change but our viewpoint. And yet, by changing our reaction to the situation, we eliminate the problem: we cease to resist it. Things may be at their worst and we remain happy. Each time we rise above a painful situation, we have attained soul growth. Hopefully, this awareness will make future problem situations of the same kind unnecessary.

*One of the goals is
single-pointedness—
to enter into a
moment completely,
without judgment,
without blame,
without yearning—
to become so
absorbed in whatever
you are doing
that all else
ceases to exist.*

Section Three
Master of Life Teachings
In Action

There is a Zen koan that asks, "A man hangs on by one hand to a root over a sheer precipice. Can he open his grip and let go?" What a spiritual-potential seminar like the **Master of Life Training** can do is to hang a man on that precipice; but there is the root that brought him there in the first place, and to that he will cling with tenacious desperation. Only he himself can relinquish that grip when he is ready. **Master of Life** awareness gets you ready to let go, but it is you who has to let go.

The following dialogues are primarily in response to an altered-state session, an exercise, or talk. As a result of being hung over the precipice, the participant decides to question his own situation:

9.
Karen

Karen almost held up her hand. She was forcing herself to ask a question but doing it timidly, hoping that I wouldn't see her. When I called upon her, she stood up and quietly asked, "Is possessiveness considered one of the fears that must be overcome?"

"Yes. Are you possessive of your husband?" I asked. She nodded affirmatively.

"Well, we are possessive because we are insecure, and it isn't logical. Why are we insecure? Because we don't believe we will have enough. Enough what? Enough love, enough sex, enough time, enough control, enough exclusive attention ... or maybe we're afraid the relationship won't last forever. We feel something is missing or impermanent, and we don't always even know what it is, or why we feel what we feel. But we grab harder to assure nothing else is lost."

"That's just about it," Karen said. "I don't know why I fight it so much!"

"Well, it could be programming from a past life, Karen," I explained. "Maybe the two of you have been together before. Or it could be any of thousands of other reasons. Throughout our lives, we are always moving from the known to the unknown. This makes us insecure, and we fight it. We resist insecurity, but to no avail. People and circumstances will always change.

"But let's look at that," I continued. "What if you could attain **total security**? Think about it. Anyone with any sense of adventure, any drive or imagination would soon become bored. Your life would become dull and mundane. There would be no challenge in your relationships or in your life ... no aliveness. Think back on your own relationships and those you have observed. When there is no challenge and no aliveness in a relationship, it goes flat. There is no energy and pretty soon you probably couldn't care less if the relationship lasted or not."

"Then it's a double bind," she said in response. "Damned if you do and damned if you don't."

"Right," I admitted. "You are possessive because you don't want to lose the relationship. You are possessive because you are insecure. But if you were totally secure, there would be no challenge or aliveness, so you'd probably grow tired of the relationship. So your fearful emotions are **not even logical**."

Karen thought for a long time before saying, "Well, what if I said I was jealous of my husband? There are differences between possessiveness and jealousy."

"Sure, there are," I said. "When you are jealous of your husband, you are excessively concerned that he is not as committed to the relationship as you want him to be. In being jealous, your viewpoint is one of being incomplete. For some reason, you think that only through the relationship with him can you be complete. But stop, step back and look at that. You have to realize it isn't logical. If you aren't complete without your husband, the relationship cannot make you complete. Excessively jealous people often feel that they won't be able to survive without the other person. And that isn't any more logical than the first point I made. You know you'll survive, but your jealousy could drive your husband away, because jealousy is always **hostility** with a mask."

"Oh, boy!" Karen said, sitting down.

"We'll be exploring a lot more that directly relates to your situation, Karen. Stay with me. And be aware that most of your fears are just as illogical as those we just explored."

Whenever you act with intention, you create karma, because all such acts are motivated by hatred or desire (even if it is the desire to do good).

9.
Rosemary

"Aren't you overlooking something?" Rosemary asked, with noticeable anger in her voice. "Maybe Karen has damn good reason to be jealous and possessive of her husband. Maybe her husband, like mine, can't be trusted out of her sight."

"You can't change other people, Rosemary. It never works. Oh sure, you can tell your husband, 'If you don't change, I'm going to leave.' And the threat might even work for a while. But then he'd be repressing what he really wants to do, and eventually the repression will erupt, maybe in an even less desirable way."

"Oh, great! I can look forward to living like this for the rest of my life. I came here to find answers on how to make it work, not to hear that," she snapped.

"I don't have anyone else's answers, Rosemary," I responded. "What I can do is create the space for you to find your own answers. You need to be aware that you cannot change others, so you might as well accept them as they are, if you choose to remain in the environment. I take it you want to stay with your husband. But what if you knew that, after another ten years, things would still be the same between the two of you. Would you stay?"

"No way," she replied.

"What about five years?" I asked.

"No!" she said.

"Two years?"

Rosemary looked away, thinking for several seconds. "Uh huh, I'd stay two more years."

"All right, at least we're getting somewhere. Your marriage is terminal. He has two years to change. Do you really think he'll change?"

"I doubt it. He'll probably be an old man before he stops chasing around," she said sadly.

"What if you were to change, Rosemary. You can't change your husband, but you can change yourself and then he'd be reacting to a new person in you. He might change because **he** wanted to."

"Do you mean be nicer to him or be more sexy ... or something like that?" Rosemary asked.

"I don't know how you might change, because I don't know the inner workings of your relationship. But what about that? What if you were nicer and sexier?"

"No, it isn't that we don't get along. We get along great most of the time. And our sex life is great. It's just that he likes variety. And that is something I can't provide."

"Okay, let's look at it from another viewpoint. Your husband's affairs are fulfilling some psychological needs he has. Would he be open to exploring his own insecurities in a seminar like this or with a psychologist or psychiatrist?"

"You don't know how funny that question is, Richard. Absolutely not. Without going into details, absolutely not."

"Well, then, that's what is. What is, is your husband is a man who likes to chase around and have affairs with other women. And what is, is he probably isn't going to change. And what is, is you're going to stick around for another two years. So, my advice to you is to accept him as perfect the way he is."

"What?!" Rosemary almost screamed at me.

"In accepting what is, you can find some peace. Don't be blind to the logic. It isn't logical to upset yourself when there is no value in doing so. The upset will only result in more negative programming of your subconscious mind, so it will only make matters worse.

"Think about it, Rosemary," I continued. "Since you can't change him, unless you can come up with some other creative solution, you might as well give him the freedom to be what he is."

61

"What do you mean by some other creative solution?" she asked.

"In twenty years of working with people, I've seen and heard about some pretty unusual arrangements that work for those involved. Open sexual agreements, threesomes, and group sex are ways some people resolve their needs. There are as many potential arrangements as there are people."

"No, I've thought about that, and we even tried something once, but I have no desire for further experimentation in that area," she explained.

"All right, then you really have only two choices. You can choose to remain in the environment or leave. And you can choose to resist what your husband is or accept him as perfect. If you accept him as he is, then let go of your anger, resentments, hostility and blame. Unless you let go of the negative emotions, you'll still be resisting him."

"Some choices," Rosemary quipped. "And there is no way I'll ever look at him as perfect."

"Then how about replacing 'perfect' with 'acceptable as he is'?" I asked.

Rosemary gave me an exasperated look and sat down.

*Life becomes
unnecessarily difficult
only when you attempt to transform what is,
into what you want it
to
be.*

10.
Joan

"I think it is ridiculous to say that someone is acceptable as they are when they are behaving badly,"

62

Joan said, holding the hand of her husband, Dave, who remained seated beside her. She was in her late thirties with short hair, dressed in a conservative pantsuit.

"Then you've missed the logic of what I just shared," I said.

"No, I didn't!" she responded. "I just cannot imagine sitting back and accepting adulterous behavior."

"Rosemary is free to leave," I said. "Since she doesn't want to do that, she is then free to resist or not resist her husband. Her resistance will program her subconscious negatively, resulting in future negativity that will have to come out. Is that what you advocate?"

"Yes, her husband is wrong!"

"So, even if you make your own life more miserable, you'd choose anger and hostility?"

"Yes, as a matter of pride," she said, glancing down at Dave, who was quick to nod his approval.

"Pride is responsible for more misery than any other emotion. When you say pride, you mean standing up for what is 'right.' And the usual result is you get to be right and you lose the game. You're certainly not alone in your opinion. It's the choice most people make every day. And it certainly isn't unconditional love."

"What's wrong is wrong!" Joan said, raising her chin a little higher. Dave nodded, this time all on his own.

"What's wrong is wrong to you, Joan and Dave ... and is not necessarily what is wrong to me," I replied.

"Well, if you're going to put yourself above society ..." Joan began.

"JOAN! Get off it! Are you and Jerry Falwell here on earth to tell us what is right and wrong?"

Joan was obviously furious, and Dave was wishing he could crawl under the chair. "Don't put me in the same category with Jerry Falwell," she sputtered. I just looked at her for several seconds without saying a word. She sat down and looked at Dave, who wasn't looking at anyone.

63

"Joan, I'm talking to you, and everyone else in this room. There are no such things as right and wrong, moral and immoral, ethical and unethical. A group of people agree upon terminology and maybe they agree to call a particular action right. That doesn't make it right. That only makes it what one group of people **calls** right. It certainly doesn't change what actually is. Concepts of right and wrong have swung like a pendulum throughout history and they change, depending upon when and where you live. In some countries, eating cattle is the ultimate immorality. In other countries, the word 'rape' is not a part of the language, or even a concept, for men assume the right to take women by force whenever they want to. In several areas of the world, open sexuality is encouraged. Right, wrong, moral, and immoral are all concepts which exist only by agreement of a group of people.

"Living in a society, we must be willing to accept the consequences of our actions regarding the laws of that society," I continued. "Yet most of the conflicts with the opinions of other people are not legal issues. So, it may be ill advised to allow what other people think to cause you to repress what you really are."

"But sin is sin!" Joan interrupted. "It's against God, and you are sounding more like the devil every minute."

"I am whatever you think I am, Joan. I couldn't be anything else to you. Again, that's just basic logic," I replied.

"You're just a ... a ... liberal!" Dave sputtered, without standing.

"I believe in liberalism but not the devil, and what I am to you is what is for you. But let's get back to sin ... awful SIN. Do you know the original definition of the word 'sin'? It meant 'missing the mark.' Sounds to me almost like generating disharmonious karma. You missed it this time, but you might get it right next time.

64

"The organized religions and churches have created sin as you think of it. Did you know that in twelfth-century England, thinking about sex was considered a sin, even if you were married? How about that, Joan and Dave? The missionary position was the only acceptable coital position, and only for the purpose of begetting children. Sex was totally forbidden on Sundays, Wednesdays, Fridays and for forty days before Christmas or Easter.

"In England, from A.D. 800 to A.D. 1000, celibacy was considered unhealthy and prostitution was whole-heartedly supported by the populace and the authorities. At this time, public nudity was accepted at beaches and women were free to take lovers regardless of their marital status.

"In ancient Sparta, the public nudity of both young men and women was encouraged. Young people experienced sexual freedom before marriage, as celibacy was considered a crime. It was also acceptable for older men to 'loan' their wives to relatives or friends for the purpose of bearing a child if the combination might result in a superior human specimen.

"In Greece, homosexuality was not only acceptable but was regarded as the highest form of love. The courtesans of Greece received more education, freedom and respect than other women of their time.

"I could go on and on, Joan and Dave. I've been exploring this idea of sin for a long time and I have to simply take it back to harmonious or disharmonious karma."

"Thou shalt not commit adultery!" Joan said loudly. "That is a sin and none of your fancy words or rationalizations can make it into anything else."

"Well, the subject is covered under the second pillar of dharma in Buddhist teachings. It is one of the points in the field of purifying action, and is interpreted as refraining from those actions of sensuality which cause pain and harm to others, or turbulence or disturbance in ourselves.

"If you were to explore the Six Paramitas of the Bodhisattva (A.D. 400–500) you would find adultery is one of the precepts. And it is explained as meaning that the person having sex with another must consider his own happiness, that of his companion and of the third person who will be most affected by his action. If these three concerned people can be satisfied, then the sex act comes under natural law and is completely acceptable.

"Your thinking is restrictive, Joan. Do you know why?" I asked.

"It is not restrictive! It is moral and spiritual," she responded, standing once again. "Obviously, this is a gathering of heathens!"

"Heathens? Joan, how about doing a quick regression? Are you open to explore why you feel so strongly about this subject?"

She hesitated, looking at Dave, who was fixedly contemplating the design in the carpet.

"Come on out to the aisle, Joan," I said, and she responded. [**Note:** Participants are conditioned in the beginning of the seminar to respond instantly to an altered-state suggestion. This allows me to individually regress participants quickly into their past, either in this life or a previous one. A support team member assists in the process and the participant is often regressed standing up. In this situation, I touched Joan on the forehead, activating the past programming suggestion, counted her down into the altered state and gave her suggestions.]

"All right, Joan, you have very strong feelings about morality, right and wrong, and sexual misconduct. So, I want you to go back into your own past to find the cause of these feelings. Everything we feel strongly about relates back to an event or series of events that transpired in the past ... the past of this life, or in a previous incarnation. And now, I'm going to count backward from five to one, and on the count of one, very strong impressions will come in that relate to your feelings about morality and sexual misconduct. You are going back to the cause of these feelings ... number five ... number four ... number three ... number two ... number one. You are now there and the impressions are beginning to form. Please speak up and tell me what you perceive. What is happening?"

"I'm just watching this man, he's dressed like medieval England or Europe. He's very sad. Very upset. Maybe ... I can't tell if he's sad or mad. I guess both."

"Is the man you?" I asked.

"Ah ... I don't know ... yes, I think it is. A man, my God, a man!" she said, amused and astonished at the same time.

"All right, now, why is he sad?"

"I don't now," she responded. "But he seems angrier now, he is throwing things ... kitchen things."

"Yes, you do know why he is mad, and I want you to move backward in time, just far enough to find out what happened. On the count of three, you'll be there and vivid impressions will begin to come in. One , two, three."

"Oh, he has just found out that his wife has left him. (Brief pause.) Yes, my wife has gone off with another man ... the man who worked in the bakery." (Joan began to swear, exhibiting extreme agitation.)

"All right, let go of this. Let's move on to a time a few weeks after your wife left you. On the count of three, you'll be there. One, two, three."

"Bitter, I'm very, very bitter. I hate her! She ruined my life, ruined everything. Ruined, ruined, ruined."

"What did you do to cause her to leave you?" I asked.

"Absolutely nothing. I was a good provider, she did as she was told, and we got along well."

"She did as she was told? What did you tell her to do?"

"Everything! Everything! It's a husband's right," she said in an angry tone. (Obviously, as the regression continued, Joan had moved from the position of observing to reliving the situation.)

"Is it the custom of your time? Do all husbands tell their wives what to do?" I inquired.

"No, but I do, and my father always told my mother what to do. You need order in life. Without order, what do you have?"

I continued to question Joan, and her answers provided me with the picture of an intolerant man who had driven his wife away and refused to accept any responsibility for her actions. He spent the rest of his life in bitterness, blaming her immorality for his misery. Before awakening Joan, I instructed her to move into her Higher-Self for an overview of the past lifetime. "Do you know the entity who was your wife in the past life in your current life?" I asked.

"Yes!" she replied.

"Who is it?"

"Dave."

I glanced over at Dave. His eyes fixed steadily on the carpet, he slowly nodded his head affirmatively.

11.
Neal

"What do you think about Joan's experience?" I asked the group. Neal put up his hand, and when recognized, asked "What is the value in her knowing all that?"

"Joan's conscious and subconscious mind have been out of alignment, causing her to be very judgmental. Her past experiences have generated fears that have blocked her from expressing unconditional love. Understanding your fears is one way of rising above them."

Neal seemed to ponder the answer for a while. He was in his early twenties, and dressed in a sweater and jeans. "What are other ways to rise above your fear?" he asked.

"Well, to begin with, you must realize that every problem is rooted in fear. Most of the powerful new therapies do not believe in mental illness, but contend that unhappy and neurotic people are not satisfying their needs and that they have developed negative patterns of thinking and acting. This results in anguish and suffering for them, and usually for those close to them.

"There is no way to heal a mind, so medical therapy does not relate. What is needed is an understanding of the fears behind the negative thoughts and actions, and an understanding of the individual's needs. This is followed by re-education, which is learning the skill of choosing wisely between behavior that will result in **harmony**, opposed to behavior which will result in **disharmony**. Basically, this is the ability to **reason**.

"So, if your life isn't working; if you have symptoms such as depression, anxiety, phobias, and stomach ulcers; if you drink or do drugs to escape; if you're experiencing guilt, repression, jealousy, possessiveness, hatred, anger, tension, greed, inhibition, stress, envy or paranoia ... you are experiencing irrational fears and your essential needs are not being fulfilled. The list of symptoms is endless, but whatever they are, you can help yourself to resolve them."

"But what about Joan? Her problem went back to a past life," Neal asked.

"The past life may have been the cause, but the need relates to love," I replied. "All human beings have the same physiological and psychological needs, but we vary in our ability to fulfill them. Psychiatry is concerned with two basic psychological needs: 1. the need to love and be loved, and 2. the need to feel worthwhile to

69

ourselves and to others.

"Regarding the need to love, you must be involved with other people—one person at the very minimum. We all must have one person who loves us and whom we love. If we don't have this critical person in our life, we will not be able to fulfill our basic needs, and mental symptoms will result.

"Regarding the need to feel worthwhile to yourself and to others, you must maintain a satisfactory standard of behavior. This means that you must correct yourself when you are wrong. If your conduct is below your standard, you must correct it or you will suffer, just as if you had no one to love and to love you.

"This is why much of this seminar is about exploring your fears and working to remove the blocks to your expression of unconditional love. It is also about exploring your behavior to decide if it is disharmonious and if you need to change it.

"I encourage immediate changes in **behavior** which will quickly lead to a change in **attitude**, which can lead to fulfilling your needs. **You don't have to change how you feel about something to affect it if you are willing to change what you are doing**. Change begins with action. Karma is action, and wisdom erases karma.

"And remember what I said earlier: Nothing about ourselves can be changed until it is first recognized and accepted. So, to recognize what you really are behind all your masks, you must ask yourself a lot of questions. Answers are never difficult if you stop avoiding the questions you need to ask yourself. So, in regard to any fear area, there are four questions:

1. What is the real fear?
2. What needs do I have that are not being met?
3. What am I doing that creates disharmony?
4. How can I change my behavior to create more harmony?

"Okay, what about resistance?" Neal asked. "Back when you were talking about resisting what is, I realized that I resist my boss something terrible. I mean, everything he says just grates on me. I dwell on it. I just hate him for some reason and I don't even know why."

"All right, Neal, close your eyes and just trust the first thoughts that come into your mind. What is the real fear behind your resistance to your boss?"

"I don't know," he immediately replied.

"Yes, you do, Neal, and you're not playing the game. Just trust the thoughts that come in."

"That he'll win!" Neal blurted out, loudly.

"What does that mean?" I asked.

"Well, he's just so damned smug. He's such a know-it-all, always looking down his nose at me. If I didn't do something, he would think that he is superior! And he isn't—he's an idiot!"

"So the fear is that you'll lose because you didn't get to be right, and get to be superior over him?" Neal grimaced at the way I viewed his response. "All right, Neal, second question: What needs do you have that are not being met?"

"Ah, I'd like some respect for my abilities. All I ever get from him is disapproval."

"Neal, any time you or anyone else gets upset with anyone about anything, your expectations are in conflict with **what is**. You have expectations of approval or control, and when these expectations aren't fulfilled, you get upset. You want to attain your boss's approval or control his actions. Neither is your right. And what is, is that your boss is a superior acting know-it-all! Okay, third question: What are you doing that creates disharmony?"

"I verbally cut at him whenever I can, in areas that don't contradict his authority. I keep it personal, that way he can't get me fired for my attitude toward my work," he said, with obvious pride

"Okay, Neal, last question: How can you change your behavior to create more harmony?"

"Well, I guess I could let him be right and just do my job. I could just accept that he is what he is. From what I've heard in here, I'm just making it worse by resisting because I'm programming my subconscious negatively."

"What about that?" I asked.

"Well, I guess it isn't logical to make things worse for yourself. It's kinda dumb, too."

Turning to the rest of the participants, I said, "So the idea here is **conscious detachment based upon awareness ... based upon wisdom.** And I contend that once Neal changes his behavior, he will soon change how he feels about his work relationship. He may not ever like his boss, but his boss will cease to be an issue. Remember, a change in behavior will quickly lead to a change in attitude. You don't have to change how you feel about something to affect it if you are willing to change what you are doing."

Dharma is your duty to yourself and society. Your karma conditions you through your experiences to create the character to carry out your dharma.

12.
April

"I'm still stuck on some of the things you said about accepting other people as they are. Some people just aren't acceptable as they are," April stated, making gestures of futility with her hands. She was in her late twenties, attending the seminar with a girlfriend who apparently shared her taste for trendy attire.

"April, when you can't accept someone as they are, you are making them wrong in comparison with your viewpoint. And that is not unconditional love. You also need to be aware that you don't see the other people in your life as they really are. You see them through your veil of opinions and conclusions ... your totally subjective viewpoint. So, you certainly don't see them accurately.

"Remember back to when a friend fell in love with someone, and you could not understand what she saw in him? Well, your viewpoints were different. Everybody sees everybody differently, and none of these perceptions are accurate. Thus we all deal with illusions. **Illusions!**

"Other people's reactions to you are nothing but statements of their viewpoints, and they have nothing to do with accurate facts and absolutely nothing to do with the way things actually are. So, if human interaction is based upon perceptions that are inaccurate, that are illusions, then why bother to judge others at all? It isn't even logical.

"And when you stop judging other human beings, you let go of another fear and you become capable of expressing more unconditional love."

"Okay," April said, bouncing back into her seat.

73

13.
Warren

Warren was in his mid-thirties, dressed in tan slacks and a pin-striped, button-down shirt with the sleeves rolled up. He wore his hair in a conservative businesslike style, short and trimmed around the ears. "Several times you've talked about how it is impossible to change other people, but it seems to me that you are being unrealistic in this area. Life is about influencing others. You certainly do your part by writing books and conducting seminars like this."

"Warren, I say that if you force the other person to repress what they really are, it won't work. Their repression will just surface in other, possibly less desirable ways. We are all free human beings and should be respected for what we are, not for what someone else wants us to be. Of course, there is nothing wrong with attempting to influence others. We all do this all the time. Nearly everything we say is an attempt to influence others, even if we are simply attempting to influence them to listen to us.

"When you attempt to force another person to change, you make a mistake. Exceptions to this might be situations of physical abuse, alcoholism or drug addiction. In such extreme situations, the only way to be responsible to yourself might be to remove yourself from the environment you find yourself within."

14.
Michelle

Michelle was attractive, about fifty years old, and appeared to be attending the seminar alone. She wore no wedding ring and was dressed in expensive casual attire. "In the 'back to the cause' regression we just completed, I experienced something I'm having a difficult time figuring out," she said.

74

"What were you investigating?" I asked.

"Well, I'm a workaholic," she responded. "I've always figured I worked for the prestige that accompanied success. You now, the old ego story. And, as a secondary reason, I figured it was a great way to hide from social involvement I didn't enjoy. But now I'm wondering if maybe I just do it because I'm greedy—because I want to accumulate more and more things and a bigger and bigger bank account."

"Do you enjoy the fruits of your accomplishments?" I asked.

"Not really," she said. "My only enjoyment seems to be in accumulating more."

"Greed is preparing to live as opposed to living now," I said. "A truly fearless person is never greedy. But tell me about your regression."

"I was a dirt-poor Hispanic. Nothing exciting happened, and I don't even know for sure where I lived, but the visual impressions were very vivid. They came in flashes. First, I seemed to be a young woman. The house I was in was only about ten feet square, just made of sticks tied or braided together. It was hardly any protection at all. The floor was dirt and there were a couple of makeshift cots and cardboard boxes containing clothes. I cooked on an open fire outside. Then the next flashes were of being in a church—a Catholic church. And I seemed to be enchanted by the beautiful artifacts. Outside was a little village and most of the houses were like mine. There was a horse and wagon in the street and the impression I had was that it was around the turn of the century. So the question I'm asking myself is, 'Am I a workaholic today because I had so little in a past life?'"

"I don't know, Michelle. You're asking yourself the first of the four questions: What is the real fear? Would you like to explore it in more detail?"

Michelle indicated that she wanted to continue the exploration, so I touched her on the forehead, counted her into a deep, altered state of consciousness, and gave her these instructions: "You are very deep and relaxed and at ease, and I now want you to move up into the very highest level of your mind, into the superconscious Higher-Self. From this level, you will have access to all knowledge of the past life as the Hispanic woman and how she relates to your present obsession with material gain."

Michelle was then directed into the Higher-Self. "I want you to let the impressions form," I said. "Ask for the awareness we are seeking and when you are ready, please speak up and explain to me how your past life relates to your present life."

She was silent for two or three minutes before speaking. "I lived with my husband in the house I described. We had nothing but each other. He was very good-looking and ... oh." She was silent again for a while. "He was attracted to another woman. She didn't live in our village, but when he went off with the others to work, he sometimes worked on the land of her family. They were very wealthy. He left me for her." A tear began to roll down Michelle's face and I used a tissue handed to me by the support team member to wipe it away.

"How does this relate to your present life, Michelle?" I asked.

"I don't like what I'm getting," she said sadly, shaking her head.

"Please tell me."

"I've got it all turned around. I've been wasting my whole life over this ... this ... I don't believe it! **If I become rich, then I'll attract a husband like she did,**" she said loudly and began sobbing.

"All right, Michelle, on the count of five you will awaken, remembering absolutely everything you just

76

experienced. You'll awaken, thinking and acting with calm self-assurance, at peace with yourself, the world and everyone in it. One, two, three, four, five. Wide awake."

Michelle opened her eyes, looked at me sadly and then at the floor. "I've always kept men at arm's length and told myself, 'Once I've made it, there will be plenty of time for men.' Well, look at me. I'm fifty-two years old and a ten-year-old cat is the only thing on earth that loves me."

"All right, I think you understand the **false fear karma** you're experiencing, Michelle. You consciously know that love is not dependent upon wealth, but your subconscious mind was programmed with that fear. The traumatic past-life incident generated a fear that is not valid in the context of your current life."

"But it has ruined my life," she blurted out.

"**It is you,** Michelle. You've always had the free choice to accept the fear or confront it. Courage is the willingness to be afraid and act anyway. You could have feared love without being wealthy, but acted anyway and taken a chance. And you still can. Fifty-two isn't very old, and I'm going to be hokey enough to say, 'this is the first day of the rest of your life.'"

She smiled at me, obviously appreciating my words.

"Michelle, let's go on to the next three questions. Number two is: What needs do you have that are not being met? Obviously, the answer to that is the need for love. Number three is: What are you doing that creates disharmony?"

"Well, I don't see it as disharmony," she replied. "But when I reject every man I meet, I guess it doesn't create harmony. I suppose I could be receptive. Simple, huh? But I haven't been before. It just wasn't in me to be receptive. Maybe it never will be."

"I doubt that, Michelle. False fear and false guilt karma are the easiest to overcome. But let's look at

77

question number four: What immediate actions can you take to create harmony?"

Before she could answer, another participant, a man of about sixty, who was seated a couple of rows in front of Michelle, stood up. "She could start by having dinner with me," he said, winking at her.

"You're on," she responded, smiling back at him.

> *A Master of Life isn't an ordinary human being with something added, but is rather an ordinary human being with his irrational fears taken away.*

15.
Sunny

As Sunny spoke, she began rubbing the back of her neck, which is body language indicating anxiety related to her words. She was in her mid-twenties, dressed in jeans and a white cotton beach jacket with the collar turned up. "I've been forced, through a shifting of assignments in my office, to work with a woman who drives me to distraction. She isn't superior to me nor am I to her, but she acts like she is the boss. She does everything she can to put me down and to discredit me to our boss. She's several years older and I'm afraid she is going to hurt my career in the film business."

"How do you respond to her?" I asked.

"I try to keep it in and remain perfectly nice. Just like the mask you talked about. And I've listened to everything that has been said in this seminar, and I know a lot of it applies to this situation, but I just don't see how the awareness is really going to change anything."

"What is it you see in her that you recognize as existing within yourself?" I asked.

"What? Nothing! There is nothing about her that I see in myself," Sunny responded.

"Sunny, there is a human-potential concept called 'the mirror.' It is used in many trainings and some mental health counselors even use it as the basis of their practice. The mirror can be approached in several ways: 1. That which you resist and react to strongly in others is sure to be found within yourself; 2. That which you resist and react to in others is something you are afraid exists within you; 3. That which you resist in yourself, you will dislike in others."

"It certainly doesn't apply in my case," Sunny said sarcastically.

"Maybe not, Sunny, but let's look for reflections anyway. What quality do you dislike most in this woman you work with?"

"She's deceitful. Last week she took a research report out of my desk, read it, then discussed it with our boss before I even presented it to him. When I did, it was anti-climactic because he was already aware of the information."

"Okay. How are you deceitful in your life, Sunny, and with whom?"

"I don't think I am deceitful," she replied. "I hate deceit."

"I realize that, otherwise you wouldn't react so strongly. And it's time to be straight, Sunny. How are you deceitful and with whom?"

She scowled at me, looking directly into my eyes. I stared back just as directly. "I guess I have been deceitful with my boyfriend the last couple of months. I'm kind of in a quandary because I met someone else at work and I really like him. We have lunch together almost every day. I went out with him once while John was fishing with his friends. Are you saying that because I'm having a hard time with myself over that, I'm having a hard time with Mary at work?"

"I don't know, Sunny. Is that it?"

She didn't respond.

"There's one more aspect to the mirror concept, and that is, you become what you resist."

Sunny sat down, rubbing her neck a little harder.

16.
Aura

I was talking to the entire group about guilt. "Guilt is not just something that happened in the past. Everyone in this room is dealing with different kinds of guilt. Guilt is the primary manipulation trap that people use on each other, especially within families and close relationships. There are only two reasons for someone to attempt to make you feel guilty: 1. to control you; 2. to hurt you. Neither is worthy of your consideration. Here are a few of my favorite lines: 'How can you treat me like this?' 'It was your fault that I was upset and didn't get enough sleep!' 'I've been waiting by the phone all week for you to call.' And if you feel guilty, don't blame them. Blame yourself for allowing someone to manipulate you.

"It's easiest to break guilt down into three kinds: 1. current guilt; 2. long-standing guilt; 3. philosophical guilt. Examples of current guilt might be not spending enough time with the kids or not calling your parents as often as you feel you should. Examples of long-standing guilt would be guilt over leaving your ex-wife, or guilt over refusing to allow your ailing father to move in with you when he asked to. An example of philosophical guilt would be not tithing to the church when you feel it is your responsibility to do so.

80

"Guilt is an attempt to make right in the present something you did or think you are doing wrong. Guilt always inhibits you and you dwell upon the guilt, generating more and more negative programming to your subconscious mind each time you think about it.

"But let's deal with the guilts one at a time. Since no one can change the past, long-standing guilt is always inappropriate. You can't undo what is done, and to dwell upon it destroys the present and future. But current guilt and philosophical guilt you can do something about if you choose to. You choose guilt to support a viewpoint of being bad. You want to gain self-acceptance and you can't do this when you feel you are bad, unless you make yourself feel guilty. Guilt is an internal debit and credit system. Once you've felt guilty long enough, it balances or justifies your actions. You can feel okay with yourself. The problem is that you usually just do the same thing all over again. Guilt is often a never-ending spiral unless you decide to end it. From a karmic perspective, guilt is one of the most destructive of all emotions."

Aura was a very pretty woman in her late thirties, dressed in a long cotton dress in a style that had been popular with the hippies in the 60's and early 70's. She wore several kinds of metaphysical necklaces around her neck and silver and turquoise bracelets on both arms. "I'd like nothing more than to let go of the guilt that haunts me, but how do you do it?" she asked.

"It has to start with an awareness of guilt and how it works," I said. "Then, if it's a current or philosphical guilt, you're going to have to explore the clarity of your intent. In other words, decide what is important and act. If your guilt is long-standing and you cannot do anything to remedy the situation, label it 'experience,' file it away and go back to it only as a point of reference."

"But I can't let go of it. My guilt is long-standing and haunts me night and day. When I was younger, I took a lot of drugs. Four years ago, my daughter was born mentally retarded. Every day she is a living reminder of my guilt. I love her more than anything in the world, and I've rearranged my whole life to take care of her. But when I think about how I robbed her of the life she could have had, it just kills me." Tears were rolling down Aura's cheeks and she couldn't hide her trembling.

"Aura, did you know when you took the drugs that they would someday affect a child you might have?" I asked.

"No, I didn't. I really didn't," she responded. "But I certainly should have considered the possibility."

"Aura, you have an understanding of karma. It is never one-sided. The soul that entered your daughter's body deliberately chose the circumstances as a way to resolve her own karma, and to offer you the opportunity to resolve yours."

"If only I could believe that," she said.

"Do you accept karma as what is?" I asked. She nodded. I continued, "Then you have to accept that there is no halfway karma. **All** is karma or this is a random universe and there is no meaning to life other than what you see. Would you like to explore your relationship in regression?"

"Oh, yes, please," she said.

After inducing an altered state of consciousness, I told Aura, "Somewhere in the memory banks of your subconscious mind are memories that relate to your current situation with your daughter. And I want you to let go of the physical and flow back into your mental memories of previous incarnations to observe firsthand how the past relates to the present. It is time to attain an awareness of the karmic relationship, and to better understand that which influences, restricts, and motivates you now."

I gave Aura the regression instructions, then said, "The impressions are beginning to form. When you can, I want you to speak up and tell me what you perceive."

"Riding on horseback ... going very fast. There's a man in a uniform of some kind and ... oh, no! Somebody shot him. He's fallen off the horse and is just lying there, not moving. Other riders are coming; they are dressed in different uniforms. They look at him and laugh, and just ride away."

"Are you the man who has been shot?" I asked.

"I think so."

"Let's move forward in time until something else happens, if it does. On the count of three, you'll be there. One, two, three. What's happening now?"

"Someone else, another man in the same kind of uniform as mine. He's helping me. The bullet wound is to the left side of my stomach and he is attempting to stop the bleeding. He seems to be wounded, too, but he is putting me on the horse now, taking me somewhere."

"All right, let's move forward in time until we can find out how this comes out. Move to an important situation in the future. One, two, three."

"I'm in a bed in the ward of an old-fashioned hospital. A nurse is telling me I won't ever be able to walk again. The bullet hit my spine and my legs are paralyzed. My friend—the one who saved me—is there too. Oh, God, I'm just going crazy. I'm screaming at them to shoot me right now and put me out of my misery. The nurse doesn't care. She's just watching and then she just walks away." Aura breaks off for a moment, tears slipping down her cheeks. Sobbing, she continues, "My friend says he'll help me. His parents have a farm and we'll go there."

"All right, I want you to let go of this. Now, on the count of three and not before the count of three, without pain and without emotion, I want you to move forward to a time a few weeks before you died in this past life we are now examining. You will not yet have crossed over into spirit. It will be a few weeks prior to your death. And I want you to attain an overview of all

83

that happened of importance up to this time. One, two, three."

Aura was silent for a moment or two, her eyes moving rapidly under her closed lids, an indication that dream-like impressions were taking place. "I'm much older now and in a wheelchair in a studio-like room. Clay is everywhere—clay molds, dishes, cups, figures. Why, yes, I've learned pottery. I'm a potter, that's what I do. Funny, my hair is white at the temples and I'm probably about fifty years old. I seem to cough a lot."

"What happened to your friend, the one who saved you?" I asked.

"Hollis is here. Probably in the next room or outside," she replied.

"Then he stayed with you and helped you all these years?"

"Oh, yes, we're still on the farm. His parents died and now he runs it with his own children. But he has always helped me. I learned to be a potter and my work sells well. I help out in that way." She was silent again for a while, then said, "Hollis is Marie, my daughter."

After awakening Aura, I said, "Can you understand now, Aura? Your daughter took care of you in a previous life, and in this life, you have been given the opportunity to repay an old debt."

"Yes, I see that," she responded. "But she didn't shoot me in the past life. In our present situation, I took the drugs and she is suffering."

"Aura, from a karmic perspective, if there is karma resulting from the drug taking, you are certainly paying it off every day of your life, considering your situation with your daughter. But it was also the drug taking that set up the circumstances for mental retardation. This may be why your daughter chose to come through you. Her need to experience this tragic circumstance is due to her desire for spiritual growth, which will result from this form of balance."

"Like what? How can you possibly justify such an idea?" she asked.

"Karma is never one-sided, Aura. As Kahlil Gibran said in *The Prophet*, 'The murdered is as guilty as the murderer.' There is no way for us to know the karmic implications."

"Well, can you just make something up that could help me understand?" she almost begged.

"All right. Let's say that the soul currently inhabiting your daughter's body has become very proud over a series of lifetimes, so proud that it is detrimental to spiritual growth. Maybe the soul has been open to helping others in many lifetimes, such as the one you just explored. But this soul has grown far too proud to personally accept help from others. How does the soul regain balance? Maybe by coming into a life of total dependency. That is one potential.

"Do you see? It could be any of millions of potentials. Maybe in a past life, the soul turned away from someone in a similar position, or maybe the soul was so fearful of mental retardation that the only way to understand and rise above the fear was to experience the affliction."

The tears were now flowing down Aura's face, faster than before. A support team member handed her a tissue. "Thank you," she whispered to me.

17.
Marianne

"I know these things, but I have a hard time detaching from negativity," said Marianne, an assertive woman in her mid-forties. "When things aren't the way I want them to be, I tend to lose my temper. I just did this with the telephone company for the third time in a month."

"Well, Marianne, maybe it was your beliefs that caused the conflict. Did you approach the phone company with a preconceived belief that they are a giant, impersonal corporation that doesn't care about your needs, just your money?"

"Sure," she replied, "plus they're incompetent."

"Then it follows, Marianne, that any action the telephone company takes that justifies your negative viewpoint is going to make you mad. Yet what would happen if your belief was that the phone company is a public service organization offering the best available phone service? You probably would have been more open-minded and less emotionally involved in the encounter. Life is a lot easier when we eliminate beliefs and expectations from our reality and simply begin to experience what is."

"I can't argue with that, but what do you do about it when you catch yourself getting angry?' she asked.

"There are certainly times when I get angry, yet I catch myself quickly. I point out to myself that my expectations are in conflict with what is, and that releases the anger. That causes me to ask myself if I'm serving myself in any way in being angry. The answer is always no."

18.
Judy

"From the perspective of karma, why would someone be homosexual?" Judy asked during an open question-and-answer session.

"Would it fall under the heading of self-punishment? I certainly can't imagine that it would be a reward."

"Every situation would be different," I replied. "Either everything is karmic or nothing is karmic. So it follows that sexual preferences are lifestyle choices which result in particular life restrictions and growth opportunities. You might choose to be heterosexual, bisexual, homo-

86

sexual or celibate, and none of the decisions would have anything to do with morality. Which choice fits your karmic configurations? Which offers the best potentials to let go of fear and to express unconditional love?"

"But would it be reward or self-punishment karma?" Judy asked again.

"Well, if the gay individual had a wonderful life and found a soulmate relationship, it would certainly be a reward in my mind, Judy. But if his sexual preference caused him a lifetime of persecution, that would say to me that he was working on something he needed to resolve. And you're expressing a lot of anxiety in your body language, Judy. Why don't you tell me how this relates to you?"

"My brother!" she said, choking back emotion. "I just found out he is gay a few months ago, and I . . . I . . . just hate him for it. He has hurt my parents terribly. He has just ruined the entire family relationship."

"Judy, he hasn't hurt you or your parents," I replied. "Evidently, you are unwilling to accept your brother as he is. It is your resistance to what is that is causing your pain."

"I don't care," she snapped. "I just can't face him. I don't ever want to see him again."

"I think that would be very sad," I said, "but if that is what you have to do, that is what you'll do. Again, if everything is karmic, then this is all part of the test you have set up for yourself. I certainly wouldn't pretend to know the inner workings of the karma, but maybe your brother needs to face this family rejection without turning bitter. Maybe he needs to continue to love you even if you and your parents reject him. In so doing, he'll pass his own karmic test."

"So you're saying I'm being tested, too?" Judy asked in a sarcastic voice.

"Of course you are. Karma is never one-sided. Everyone involved is affected and is being tested. Maybe you have to test the depth of your own love. Or maybe it involves the whole concept of judgment. I don't know. But what I do know is this: You are passing your own tests when you respond to a situation with unconditional love. Unconditional love in this situation could be described as acceptance, compassion, and support."

"I just can't do that," she said.

"Judy, I said earlier in this seminar that you become what you resist. When you can't resolve your issues in this life, from the perspective of karma, it is absolute. In other words, if you condemn homosexuals, if you hate homosexuals, if you resist homosexuals, you'll probably have to set it up so that you'll come back as a homosexual in a future incarnation."

"Oh, come on. No way. It's unnatural. It's sick. **No way!**" she almost screamed.

"Judy, do you accept karma and reincarnation as your philosophical basis of reality?" I asked.

"Yes," she said, softly this time.

"Then you know what I'm saying is what is. You've just avoided facing it until now. Let go of your judgments. Do you know that several important metaphysical gurus say that bisexuality is the norm? They say that spiritually, we are androgynous—there is no sexual difference on the other side. Thus, we are all equally male and female and when you choose to love one sex over another, you deny some part of you. They think that to be heterosexual or homosexual is to be lopsided, fixated.

"I don't know if they are right or wrong," I continued, "but I think it is stupid to teach that bisexuality is more desirable. What is desirable is that which best fits your karmic needs. So, from a spiritual viewpoint, how can one sexual preference be more desirable than another?"

"I've got to think about it all," Judy said, sitting down.

*There is a Zen koan
which describes three men
observing a flag
fluttering in the breeze:
One man says, "The
flag is moving."
The second man says,
"The wind is moving."
The third man says,
"You are both wrong; it
is your mind that is moving."*

19.
Ray

"As I listen to all the pain in this room, all the guilt and fears and unhappiness, I know I've made the right choice in deciding to remain alone. Other people, one-to-one relationships and responsibilities are always the root of the problems and conflicts and pain, so I live a hermit-like lifestyle," said Ray, a man in his late thirties or early forties, dressed in conservative slacks and a short-sleeved shirt.

"So you feel you can protect yourself from life by remaining uninvolved?" I asked.

"I can protect myself from the bullshit!" he replied.

"What if you are wasting an incarnation?"

"I doubt that!"

"Okay, do you accept that we are here on earth to learn to let go of fear and to learn to express unconditional love?" I asked.

"That makes sense. In fact, if reincarnation and karma are reality, I'm sure that's the way it is. But maybe I can learn to let go of fear all on my own, without others."

"Ray, to let go of fear and express love, you must know yourself. That's what life is all about. And to really know yourself and to experience what you are, you need relationships," I continued.

"Wait a minute," he said. "You say that to let go of fear and express love is one thing, not two. That means one goal. So I see the goal as letting go of the fears until I get to my center."

"Ray, how can you learn to let go of fear when you are so fearful that you refuse to interact with other human beings? I contend that you are already a Master of Life. Most of you in this room think you have to add something in the way of awareness to become self-actualized. I contend that it works the other way. Once you have truly let go of your fears and allowed yourself to become what you really are, you'll find that you are already a totally self-actualized, enlightened, beautiful soul—the essence of unconditional love. The problem is that, for many lifetimes, you have accepted fear programming until it surrounds your etheric body like layers of darkness. To become all you are capable of being, you must remove these layers."

"So you think I'd have to interact with others to peel away the layers?" Ray asked.

"I know it, Ray. As an example, maybe one of the fear areas you must learn to deal with is rejection. How could you learn about it on your own? Or maybe you need to learn humility, which would be rather difficult to do alone."

"Got it," he said, smiling.

20.
Marlene

Marlene was in her early forties, wearing several metaphysical symbols around her neck, and dressed in trendy new safari-style baggy slacks and an oversized shirt. "The awareness I've attained in this seminar gives me the courage to leave a repressive relationship," she said happily.

"Okay," I responded. "I take it you accept that there is no possible way to save the relationship?"

"No. To be responsible to myself, I have to leave," she said.

"How many relationships have you chosen to leave, Marlene? I'm not just talking about marriages, but also important relationships where you've lived with someone else."

She thought for a while and then said, "Seven. This is my third marriage, but I've lived with different men at different times. A couple also left me."

"Is there any pattern in why and how your relationships end?" I asked.

"Men just can't deal with an independent woman over the long haul," she laughed.

"So, what happens?"

"They become insecure and resentful because I'm the way I am."

"How are you that makes them insecure and resentful?"

"Oh, you know. I don't cheat on them, but I certainly enjoy the attention of other men. There is nothing wrong with that," she said lightly.

"Give me an example of an argument you might have with your current husband," I requested.

"Okay. Just last week, we were watching television together, and this super hunk came on the screen. I said something like, 'Wow, would I like to have a little of that,' and Jack got all pissed off. What should I have done, repressed what I thought?"

"Marlene, you didn't say that to keep from repressing, you said it to make him feel insecure. You did it purposely to hurt your husband."

"I did not!" she snapped back.

91

I just looked at her without saying anything for a long time. Then I asked the other participants, "How many in this room get that Marlene was using her casual remark as an attack?" Almost every hand went up. "Well, that's what your universe is getting," I said.

"Well, so what!" she yelled. "A man thinks that because he supports you he is the king of the gawdamn hill. It doesn't hurt to bring him down a bit."

"Marlene, nobody cares what you do. But you'd better look at your patterns of leaving. They are a direct result of your unwillingness to be responsible for your own actions. So, you can go ahead and leave because of the problems you think you have in your relationship. It's always all right to leave. And there are consequences —cause and effect. And, as you have done in the past, you'll just take your own fears and insecurities with you into the next relationship and recreate your experience all over again. You'll have another opportunity to accept responsibility for your relationships."

"So you think I'm the one at fault?"

"Hey! Once more: karma isn't one-sided. And karma either is or it isn't. It's time that every one of us on this planet accepted that the source of our unpleasant relationship experiences is always ourselves. It may go back to a previous lifetime, but the problem is always fear and the solution is always going to be love."

"Well, I don't know what I could do now. Our relationship is terrible," she sighed as she gazed fixedly down at the floor.

"What about the pattern, Marlene?"

"I guess I do make the men in my life insecure about the relationship," she replied.

"What is the real fear behind this pattern, Marlene?"

"I don't know. Maybe it is the only way I can feel superior or in control of the situation."

"All right, the next self-processing question is: What needs do you have that are not being met?"

Marlene hesitated for a long time. "What's coming in is my own need to allow others to love me. I mean I don't think I ever believed that a man could really love me. I don't see myself as very lovable. And, well, since they're just faking it to get me in the sack, I've got to get even."

"Marlene!" I said assertively.

"Oh, wow! That really is sick, isn't it? I don't even believe I just said that." She was silent for a while, then tears started to flow down her cheeks. "But it's what is going on."

"All right, Marlene, then stay with me. The third question is: What are you doing that creates disharmony?"

"That's obvious. I make men feel insecure in order to make myself feel superior."

"And the last question: How can you change your behavior to create more harmony?"

"I could work at making my husband feel more secure. I think that first, I'd have to talk to him and explain what happened here at the seminar. Then, I think I'd better work at loving myself a little more."

"What you do in life creates your self-esteem or lack of self-esteem," I said. "So, automatically, when you act more compassionately, you'll start to feel better about yourself. It's a start."

21.
Helen

"My relationship situation is different than Marlene's," Helen said. "But after that, I'm almost afraid to explore it." She was a woman, thirtyish, wearing minimal makeup and a simple cotton dress. "I'd leave my husband in a minute if it weren't for the guilt. I have so much guilt in my life already, I just couldn't deal with any more."

"I take it your husband wouldn't want a separation or

93

divorce?" I asked.

"Oh, I think he'd like it as much as I, but he won't act, either," she replied.

"What is your relationship like now?" I asked.

"Well, we don't communicate at all. We haven't slept together for over two years. Actually, we just share a house. It's a very repressive environment."

"So, what are your choices?" I asked.

"Well, I can leave and feel guilty, or I can remain in the repressive environment. Some choices," she responded.

"Or you chould change your behavior in regard to your husband. Remember, you don't have to change how you feel about something to affect it, if you are willing to change what you are doing."

"It wouldn't change anything. Nothing would change my husband," she said.

"Maybe, maybe not. But, if you change, your husband will be reacting to a new, changed person. And the bottom line is, what do you have to lose?"

"What do you mean?"

"You certainly have a no-win situation going on now. So what do you have to lose by changing your behavior? It just might change your relationship for the better. If it doesn't, maybe you can leave without feeling guilty, because you'll know you've done everything you can do. So, what do you have to lose?"

"Nothing, absolutely nothing," she responded. "And I think we've both been attempting to be 'right' for so long that we've forgotten what it would mean to win the game and make it work."

22.
Samantha

"How does abortion fit in with karma?" asked Samantha, a woman in her late twenties or early thirties, dressed in jeans and a *Save the Seals* sweatshirt.

94

"If everything is karmic and karma is never one-sided, then how does it relate to the unborn fetus? What kind of karma is the mother creating when she aborts a baby?"

"I don't think there is a general answer to that question, Samantha. Again, it would depend upon the circumstances. I could imagine a thousand responses to the question," I said.

"Please give me an example," she requested.

"Well, let's say a young woman discovers she is pregnant and doesn't want the child. She cares for the father but not enough to marry him. She doesn't believe she is old enough, or responsible enough, to care for the baby and she can barely support herself. She considers having the baby and putting it up for adoption, but she also believes that there are already too many people living on this planet. She chooses abortion as a compassionate decision. Yes, because she has acted with intention, she has created karma but it certainly wouldn't be the same karma if she had based her decision upon different circumstances and conditions. How will the karma manifest? I have no idea. Maybe she'll one day be on the other side, desiring to be born and will be aborted. I suppose that is a possibility, but I doubt that it is written.

"Karma results from intention," I continued. "So the kind of karma you create will be based upon the motive, intent and desire behind your harmonious, disharmonious or neutral actions."

"Then you don't think that abortion is always wrong?" Samantha asked.

"I've seen situations where I believe abortion was the best alternative. And I'm not into judgment," I replied. "Absolutes like right and wrong don't exist, as a famous Buddhist story demonstrates: Buddha, in an earlier incarnation, murdered a man. The man was going to murder 499 other men, and to save him from the terrible karma of murdering 499 others, Buddha took on the karma of murdering one man. In so doing, he saved the lives of the 499 men. His motives were so compassionate that his act created harmonious karma."

Samantha was quiet for a moment, thinking. Looking up, she said, "I'm pregnant and if karma is the technique we use to teach ourselves what we need to learn, what am I trying to teach myself? To be more responsible to birth control? Or is it self-punishment—the old if-you-play-you-pay bit? Or am I supposed to have a kid for some karmic reason, maybe to drive me crazy, or maybe he'd be the joy of my life?"

"No one has those answers but you, Samantha. Sadly, we learn fastest through pain. Pain is the consequence of our action. Until we learn, we continue to make the same mistakes over and over again. But when the lesson is accepted on every level of your body and mind, wisdom will have erased the karma."

"That doesn't really help me. I'm trying to decide if I should get an abortion or not, and I'm terrified of making a mistake. It's all so confused. It would be disharmonious to marry a man I don't love and who doesn't want the child. It would be disharmonious to have an abortion and feel guilty about it for years to come. And, at the same time, I don't think it would be very harmonious to have a child I didn't plan and to go through all the problems of raising it alone."

"I can't help but think that the best thing for you is to base your decision upon rising above fear and the expression of unconditional love," I said. "What is your greatest fear?"

"That I won't be able to take care of it. I do okay alone, but a child would be a real financial burden," she said.

"So, what is the worst that would happen? Would you both starve to death in the gutter?"

"No," she laughed. "I've got girlfriends who are divorced and on their own with their kids. They all make it somehow."

"So, the fear of not being able to take care of the child is a faulty assumption," I commented.

She didn't respond at first. "Maybe I'm fearful that I won't love the baby and will just be stuck with it." The other women in the group all groaned and shook their heads. "Well, I've never had a baby, I don't know that I'd automatically love it." More groans from the audience. "Okay, okay," Samantha said, feigning embarrassment with a shrug and turning her hands palms up.

"You've looked at your situation from the perspective of fear. How about from the perspective of expressing unconditional love?" I asked.

"That helps," she said, smiling more. "If I act with unconditional love, I'd probably give the kid a chance to be what he is destined to be, wouldn't I?"

"I don't know, Samantha, would you?" I asked.

"I think so," she said, nodding her head.

23.
Mark

During an open question-and-answer session in a seminar, Mark, a young metaphysical scholar, asked the following question. "Back in 1976, you wrote a book introducing the concept of parallel lives. Shortly after that, Jane Roberts came out with a book in which Seth talked about the same thing. I'm sure the publication dates of the books were too close together for either of you to have been aware of the other's work, but no one had ever talked about parallels, or separate selves before this. How do you explain it?"

"Einstein said that if he had not formulated the theory of relativity, within two years someone else was bound to have done the same work," I explained. "In other words, there was enough preparatory awareness existing as part of the collective unconscious of mankind. Ideas and insights emerge from our center at the deepest level of our unconscious mind. And, at this level, we are connected ... our consciousness is **collective**. So it almost becomes a matter of who is tuned in and looking at the right time. He'll be the one to get the idea first.

"Brad Steiger once wrote a book called **The Divine Fire**. Shortly after it was published, another man sent Brad the manuscript of an almost identical book. He'd been getting the same information and was in the process of writing it, but Brad received it first and had a publisher waiting. There are many similar stories of simultaneous discoveries in science and creative fields.

"And regarding the parallel concept: I certainly didn't see Jane's manuscript and I know she didn't see mine. What makes it even more interesting to me is that, at that time, there was no writer I admired more than Jane Roberts. She presented metaphysical concepts in a grounded, practical way."

24.
Page

I was speaking to the entire group about sub-personalities: "To achieve an awareness of your True Self, you must face the many facets of your personality, including all your sub-personalities. Through this understanding, it is easier to develop 'conscious detachment,' because you can detach from the undesirable sub-personalities by observation. Instead of being absorbed by sensations, feelings, desires and thoughts, you simply observe them objectively, without judging them, wanting to change them, or interfering with them in any way.

"Now the idea is to recognize these different aspects of yourself and let them emerge. I even like to give each sub-personality a name. In fact, here are some common sub-personalities which may help you identify your own:

The Attention Seeker	The Sympathy Seeker
The Pleaser	The Brute
The Helpless One	The Moralist
The Critic	The Aggressor
The Dominant One	The Organizer
The Sadist	The Masochist
The Sexist	The Bitch
The Drinker	The Seducer
The Complainer	The Victim
The Manipulator	The Martyr
The Nag	The Tightwad
The Romantic	The Prude
The Provider	The Entertainer
The Star	The Greedy One
The Selfish One	The Clown
The Skeptic	The Intellectual

"Everyone has some of these or other sub-personalities within him. We are all a crowd of different people jammed into one person. And often our sub-personalities are not at peace with each other. They are usually involved in a struggle for dominance."

The Master of Life Training includes group altered-state-of-consciousness processes in which I guide the participants to explore several of their sub-personalities. The instructions are as follows: "I now want you to think about one of your primary personality traits. (Period of silence.) All right, now visualize an image emerging to represent this part of you. It can be male or female, an animal, or a manifestation of your creativity. It can take any form that seems appropriate. Let the image just appear. Don't consciously attempt to form it. And once the image has taken fantasy form, give it a chance to express itself without any interference or judgment. You can even create a "thought language"

99

discussion by sending it a thought and then listening as that thought comes back to you as an answer in the form of another thought. (Period of silence.) Now, get in touch with the feelings that emanate from this sub-personality and give it a name that fits it and one which you can identify it with in the future."

After the session, I ask the participants to share what came up for them and I tell them, "When you recognize a sub-personality, you can observe it as if it were someone else ... with conscious detachment. With this awareness, if the sub-personality creates disharmony in your life, you can act by rejecting it. In your awareness of your sub-personalities, you attain mastery over them."

Page raised her hand to share. When I recognized her, she stood up and said, "The sub-personality that upset me the most is 'The Black Widow.' She appeared as a giant black spider with red lipstick and long fluttery eyelashes. Dick, when you asked in the session what causes this sub-personality to emerge and to whom does it assert itself, I saw that it emerges every time another woman comes within twenty feet of my husband. I immediately become this outwardly loving wife who almost snarls at all other females. I touch my husband, run my hands down his arms, look lovingly into his eyes and almost dare the others to get close."

"What did you get when I asked if you could associate any particular fear with this sub-personality?"

"Possessiveness, at first, but that faded out and I was left with the word 'braggadocio.' I'm not really possessive of my husband. I know he loves me and I'm quite secure in that, but I guess I take great pride in boasting that he is mine and I like to push the point. I don't know that it's harmful, but I certainly don't like this aspect of me and I believe I can detach from it in the future."

25.
Deron

In every seminar training, the basic human rights often come up in regard to various dialogues with the participants. These rights allow for expression instead of repression. A **Master of Life** grants them to all others while demanding them for himself. (Full descriptions and examples are offered in my book, **Assertiveness Training and How To Instantly Read People**.)

The Eleven Basic Human Rights

1. It is your right to do anything as long as it does not hurt someone else.
2. It is your right to maintain your self-respect by answering honestly even if it does hurt someone else (as long as you are being assertive as opposed to aggressive).
3. It is your right to be what you are without changing your ideas or behavior to satisfy someone else.
4. It is your right to strive for self-actualization.
5. It is your right to use your own judgment as to the need priorities of yourself and others, if you decide to accept any responsibility for another's problem.
6. It is your right not to be subjected to negativity.
7. It is your right to offer no excuses or justifications for your decisions or behavior.
8. It is your right not to care.
9. It is your right to be illogical.
10. It is your right to change your mind.
11. It is your right to defend yourself.

Deron looked upset with me as he rose to speak. "After all your talk about unconditional love, I'm afraid I'm having a difficult time with the right not to care."

"Deron, life is filled with thousands of 'you shoulds.' You should improve yourself. You should care about all of the charity operations. You should care about saving the whales, banning the bomb, stopping violence on TV and your friends' marital problems. The PTA thinks you should attend monthly meetings and your political party thinks you should actively and financially support their candidates. Your mother is getting old and she thinks you should be concerned about old people in general and your wife thinks you should spend more time with the kids. Your boss thinks you should spend some of your spare time doing research and your mechanic thinks you should bring your car in for service every 3,000 miles instead of every 6,000. And your mother-in-law told me she thinks you should treat her daughter a little better. Am I making my point, Deron?"

He shrugged, nodded and sat down. I continued, "There are so many 'you shoulds' that if 'you did,' you'd have no time left for anything else. You and you alone have the right to decide what to care about."

26.
Carla

"I am so afraid of failing, it almost immobilizes me," said Carla, a young woman in her early twenties who appeared to be attending the training with a boyfriend. "I'm afraid of failing in my personal life and in my career."

"How many other people in this room can identify with Carla's fear?" I asked. Over half the hands went up. "Success and failure is one of the false standards by which we measure our lives," I continued. "The way to measure your life is by your growth—not success or failure, pleasure or pain. The rich man might be very successful by worldly standards, but if he has attained no growth, his life hasn't amounted to much. The individual who has had a terrible life by worldly standards may have attained incredible soul growth, so it is he who is to be seen as an example. But back to you, Carla. What is it exactly that you fear?"

"I lie awake at nights, thinking how terrible it will be if I don't succeed in my career as a nurse. And, in my personal life, I worry about my relationship with Tom, and I'm afraid something terrible will happen and I'll lose all my possessions. I know it is irrational, but knowing that doesn't really help me."

I asked Carla if she wanted to explore her fears through regression and she readily agreed. Once the altered state of consciousness was induced, I directed her to go back to the cause of her fear: "You are now there and the impressions are forming. When you can, I want you to speak up and tell me what you perceive."

A few moments passed before Carla said, in a soft voice, "I may have sent them to their death. Oh, my God, I hope not ... I hope not."

"Tell me exactly what is happening," I said.

"I'm a young officer. This is my first test in the field. I've deployed my men into that area over there, but maybe I should have ... maybe I ... oh, no ... OH, NO!"

At this point in the regression, Carla became very upset and I directed her to let go of the past and to rise up into the Higher-Self level of mind and attain a karmic overview of exactly what happened. To condense her response, she explained that in that life, she had attended military school and, upon graduation, began to serve in the army as an officer. When sent into battle for the first time, the young man made a tactical mistake causing many men to die. Not only did he have to spend the rest of his life dealing with the guilt, but he lost his ranking and was shamed in the service. When his enlistment was up, he left the army and spent the rest of his life running from himself.

"All right, Carla, I hope you can understand how your past-life experience has programmed you with fears that do not relate to your present incarnation. Your subconscious mind is out of alignment with conscious reality, and this no longer needs to affect you. From your present level of Higher Mind, I'd like you to tell me what you can do to release your fears."

After a moment of silence, Carla answered softly, deep in an altered state of consciousness. "I must accept that my experience as the young officer related to karma I needed to experience in that time. The men who died were experiencing their own karma. I was an instrument in their death, but mine was an honest mistake and my learning balanced two lifetimes of feeling smug, self-righteous and superior to others. One of those lifetimes was as a money merchant in Mesopotamia and the other as a church bishop in Vienna in the early 1300s. From this time on, I must realize that I can let go of the effects and the fears."

[Note: Although the Higher-Self technique is usually very effective in assisting a participant to attain awareness, few people respond as quickly and accurately as Carla.]

27.
Adam

"Seek environmental harmony," I said to the group. "You can divide it into two categories: people and places. I'll begin with people. As you become more self-actualized, you'll find yourself less willing to tolerate negativity and manipulation. Thus, self-actualized people seek freeing, supportive and growth-encouraging relationships, not only with their mates, but with friends and associates as well.

"If you are currently involved in the wrong kind of relationships, you will ideally do everything within your power to improve those situations. Draw upon all of the awareness we've shared in this training room. Love and wisdom can accomplish the seemingly impossible. Self-actualization is the result of understanding, so share your **Master of Life** understanding in a non-threatening way ... with unconditional love.

"Environmental harmony in regard to place is simply a matter of seeking a place where you find more peace than anywhere else. There is a physical environment that vibrationally resonates with you. It may be where you are now, or it may be in an entirely different area of the country, or a different country. You are only a value judgment from living there now. If you're happier there, it will reflect in all aspects of your life."

Adam raised his hand to ask a question: "I'd love to move to the Florida Keys," he said. "When I'm there, I'm in harmony with the environment, myself and everyone else. But I'm a stockbroker and there are few opportunities for me to make a living there."

"I'm sure there are brokers in the Keys," I responded. "But, as I said, you are only a value judgment from living there now. Obviously, you value money more than harmony."

"No, I don't ... well, it's all I know how to do."

"And you couldn't learn to do anything else, Adam?" I asked.

"Well, I suppose I could. I hate being a stockbroker."

"How old are you, Adam?"

"Thirty-one," he responded.

"Thirty-one ... I can't imagine doing something I hated for another 34 years."

"I agree, that sounds like a bad idea," he said. "But, I mean, just pulling up stakes and leaving Philadelphia? The people I know? I'd have to give up my apartment and everything that's familiar."

"I certainly wouldn't do that to obtain harmony," I said sarcastically. "And I'm sure you'd never meet new friends in the Keys."

"Okay, I've got it," he said, sitting down.

"People find security in their insecurity," I continued. "They resist change above all else, yet it is the only thing that is assured. I'd like to share a quote by Helen Keller, and you're all aware of her handicaps. She said, 'Security is mostly a superstition. It does not exist in nature, nor do the children of men as a whole experience it. Avoiding danger is no safer in the long run than outright exposure. Life is either a daring adventure or nothing.'"

28.
Priscilla

"I've been in real estate for twenty years, but I've burned out on it," Priscilla said. "I'm ready to live dangerously, as you say, but I still can't help feeling a lot of anxiety about taking the business risk I'm considering."

"Good," I said. "If you didn't feel anxiety in regard to taking the risk, it probably wouldn't be much of a risk. You'd have already outgrown it. But there are some important questions you need to ask yourself."

"Like what?" she asked.

"First, think about the purpose of the risk. Any risk taken without a clear purpose decreases your odds. So you need to define the purpose. And the next question I'd ask myself is in regard to the fear of loss behind the risk. Generally, it will be fear of the loss of **love, control** or **self-esteem.** Which applies to your risk?

"There is another question that I always ask," I continued. "If you risk this and win, will it assist you to attain peace of mind? Maybe that is the first question we all need to ask ourselves when we are considering risk."

Priscilla was obviously considering what I'd said in relationship to her risk. I explained that the seminar included a risking process in an altered state of consciousness and it would assist her to attain additional clarity. I then explained to the group, "If your life is ever going to get better, you have to take risks. There is no way to attain growth without taking chances. And you need to be aware that not risking is often the surest way of losing, because if you don't risk, the necessity to take the chance may eventually come to you and the odds will be reduced when you are forced to act. Priscilla is burned out in the real estate business, so she is considering new career risks. This is very wise, for if she is truly burned out, she will probably begin to self-destruct her business. That's how energy works. And once you decide to take a risk, don't sit around waiting for the perfect moment to act ... because it almost never comes."

29.
Lynn

"The risk I'm considering is an emotional risk," Lynn explained. "I can see how what you just explained to Priscilla relates in some ways, but it certainly isn't the same as taking a business risk or moving to a new city."

"You're right, Lynn. An emotional risk is a risk of being honest in expressing your feelings. That's it. And when you say what you really feel, you will rise above the effects of fear."

"Yeah," she replied. "I see that."

"Are you willing to talk about the emotional risk you're considering?" I asked.

"Well, I don't know, in front of the group," she said, pausing and looking down at the floor. She was in her late twenties, very attractive and dressed in tight white jeans and a ski sweater. "Sure, I'm not ashamed of it, although society may not approve. My husband and I want to open up our relationship, sexually. You know, I mean, we really love each other, but we'd like to occasionally make love with another couple, or another individual. We're considering asking one of the men Jeff works with if he'd like to explore a threesome."

"The first question I think you should both be asking yourselves and each other is in regard to your commitment to your relationship. I've seen a lot of people use the concepts of freedom and openness as rationalizations for their failure to relate wholly to anyone."

"We've already gone through that processing," she replied. "Our commitment to each other and our relationship is number one. But we see how the old ways aren't working. Statistically, half of those who are married have had an affair and Jeff and I see that as extremely destructive. We don't think that people are inherently monogamous. I don't mean to sound like we're approching the idea as a clinical experiment. Of course, it is exciting, and we think to expand our sexual world together is the safest way. Do you think we're wrong?"

"Of course not," I responded. "And I don't think you're right, either. I just don't think there is a right or wrong in this area. The question I would ask is: Is your sexual behavior working for you? If it is and no one is being hurt, then stop worrying about what other people think.

"And you have to remember that any time you risk, you are risking loss. As I explained to Priscilla, loss of love, control or self-esteem. I think you need to look at the full potential loss in relationship to the potential gain. There are definitely possible problems. Jeff could become jealous of his friend once you begin the *menage-a-trois*. Jeff's friend could fall in love with you or you with him. You don't want to cause pain or harm to others, or create turbulence or disturbance in yourself. And, at the same time, you don't want to repress your real desires. Life isn't always simple when you consider risking."

"We've considered all those things," she said. "Are there any other questions you'd be asking yourself if you were in my shoes?"

"A few, Lynn. Do you need additional information before acting? That's a good question, especially considering the sexual diseases prevalent today. I'd also ask myself these questions: Would you be risking to please someone else? Are you afraid? If you are afraid, of what? If other people learn about your activity will they think better or worse of you and do you care what they think? If you haven't acted, exactly what fears are holding you back? Will your actions result in a more honest or freer life? Is the risk a growth step that could improve the quality of your life? Will the risk generate aliveness?"

Lynn smiled at me, nodded and sat down.

30.
Claudia

Claudia was obviously angry with me. She didn't raise her hand, but as Lynn sat down, she stood up and in a loud voice said, "How can you endorse group sex? This is supposed to be a spiritual seminar, not a hedonistic advisory meeting."

"I didn't endorse anything, Claudia. I provided Lynn with some information to assist her in finding her own answers."

"You didn't tell her she was wrong! You should have condemned her," she said, clenching her fists and scowling at Lynn, who was sitting at least twenty feet away.

"Haven't you heard anything that has been shared in this seminar room about judgment, right, wrong, moral

109

and immoral?" I asked. Claudia didn't respond but continued to stare at me, her hands planted firmly on her hips. She was about the same age as Lynn and was dressed in casual slacks and a sweater. "I'm not going to go back over all the things we've already covered, Claudia. Instead, I'm going to share some sexual facts with you.

"Sex is one of the top three issues for most people. Problems most often develop from repression in this area. People worry that they are weird ... that they are the only ones who do this or think that. And that lowers their self-esteem and makes sex a problem issue. But what I've found, as an individual counselor and in conducting seminars with almost 60,000 people, is that we all do the same things."

My notebook provided the statistics: "These are some facts about sex averaged from six different 1980's sexual studies by respected researchers. Eighty-two percent of women masturbate (they either have or they do). Eighty-three percent of men masturbate on a regular basis whether they are married or not. At least twenty percent of all women have had a homosexual experience to orgasm. One-third of all men have had a homosexual experience to orgasm. Statistics indicate a much higher percentage of people would like to have a sexual experience with the same sex but have not out of fear or lack of opportunity.

"Over one-third of all married women have had an affair and only a small percentage of these were because of deep emotional dissatisfaction with their husband. Over half of all married men have had an affair. One percent of women have been involved sexually with an animal. Sexual researchers such as Freud, Kinsey and many contemporary researchers claim we are inherently bisexual, and it is only the social mores and pressures that keep us from expressing it. These are just a few of the facts about what is with sex.

"And you're not abnormal if none of the statistics relate to you. You may have lived a very straight and fulfilling sexual reality and that's what is for you. It's time to unstick our sexual adherence ... our sexual 'rightness' issues and stop judging ourselves and others. It's time to ask, does what I do sexually work for me? Does it manifest love, health, happiness, aliveness and allow for full self-expression?"

Claudia was now red in the face. "Maybe we wouldn't have disgusting statistics like that if people like yourself, in a position of influence, would call a spade a spade," she sputtered.

"Do you mean like the churches have been doing for centuries, Claudia? It is that very condemnation of sex that has caused it to become the issue it is. The strategy of religions has been the repression of sexual energy. Religions are obsessed with sex because they can use it to make you feel guilty, and if they can make you feel guilty, they can control you. So what has been done in the past has resulted in repression, which is suicide, instead of expression, which is life. Isn't it time we approached the issue in a new way?"

"I'm not concerned with repression or expression or churches, or anything but spirituality," Claudia responded in a cold voice.

"All right, Claudia, let's look at it spiritually. It appears to me that in expressing your sexuality, you are expressing God-given energy. Your physical body is vibrational energy. Not several energies, but one. Maybe sexuality is a lower expression of that energy and as it transforms, it becomes spiritual. As it moves up out of your root chakra through your spleen, solar plexus, heart, throat, brow, and into your crown chakra, your energy refines and transforms. But it is the same energy in process and it cannot be transformed through repression. Repression of energy perverts it. Then an individual becomes obsessed with sex until he is allowed to express the energy. And now, Claudia, why don't you tell me why this is such an issue with you?"

"Go to hell! " she snapped, and walked out of the seminar.

There are many people who know the way, but there are few who practice it.

Zen

31.
Diana

"But don't you think a monogamous relationship with a husband or wife you really love offers the greatest potential for lasting happiness?" asked Diana, an attractive woman in her late thirties. Her long, dark hair hung almost to her waist and she was dressed in a white jumpsuit.

"Maybe it's the best answer for you, Diana, and for me ... and maybe for Sally, sitting over there ... but I don't know if it is the best answer for everyone. Among our close friends, there is only one couple we know who has only been married once and they've been together for over thirty years. They're both top professionals in their fields and have had an open marriage, much like what Lynn described, for more than 10 years. It works for them. And I've seen it destroy other relationships. Our mistake is in thinking what is right for us is right for everyone else."

"Okay, but obviously Lynn and her husband are seeking aliveness and challenge in their sexual life. I just think there are better ways to attain it," she said.

Noticing that Diana was wearing a wedding ring, I asked, "What do you and your husband do to create aliveness and challenge in your relationship?"

"We have an exciting sex life," she said, smiling shyly. "But I think that sexual energy can also be expressed as creativity. We do many creative things together, our favorite being a life drawing class we attend two nights a week. Then, at home, after the kids are in bed, we take turns taking off our clothes and posing for each other. It's erotic and creative at the same time."

I turned to the entire group and said "All right, Diana has been willing to share her ideas and even give us an example from her life. How many of you think that getting naked and drawing each other is just too wild for you?" About half the hands in the room went up, and I turned my attention back to Diana. "See, Diana, you think Lynn's ideas go too far, but half of your universe in here thinks you're also out there on the edge."

She looked around, giggled and shrugged her shoulders.

32.
Beth

"This morning, you helped me to see how I've lived my entire life based upon what other people think. Everything else that has come up in here has only strengthened my determination to consciously detach from the fears behind the obsession. But, Richard, I don't know that awareness is enough. Intellectual knowledge does not necessarily override emotional response."

"Maybe not instantly, Beth, but it is the place to begin. And I would advise that you use programming support. You can make your own hypnosis tapes, sleep programming tapes, you can use trigger-word, posthypnotic programming [how to make your own tapes is described in detail in Dick's book, **Past Lives, Future Loves**, published by Simon Schuster Pocket Books]. Plus, I'd use behavioral therapy thought-stopping techniques. What is your greatest fear about what other people think, Beth?"

"I suppose it is the fear that people won't approve of me," she said.

"That's good, we'll use it as an example. I know from experience how powerful this technique can be. And all you need is a tape recorder and a blank tape. First, write down your fear thoughts. Then write out several statements that contradict the fears. A contradictory statement to your fear might be: 'I approve of myself and I am no longer concerned about the opinions of others!'

"Next, record your own voice beginning with the word STOP. Yell it loudly and firmly into your tape recorder. Then, in an assertive tone, speak one of the positive statements into the tape recorder. Pause for a couple of seconds and repeat the process: 'STOP!' followed by a different statement. Do this over and over until you've recorded about 10 minutes of tape.

"Next, sit down and make yourself comfortable, with your finger ready to press the play button on the tape player. Begin to deliberately think your recurring fear thoughts. Then press the play button. Your recorded voice interrupts the fear thought and provides the assertive, positive counter-programming. Stop the tape and repeat the process. Continue to do this, over and over, for 10 minutes. Repeat the procedure three or four times a day for two weeks. After that, use the technique for 10 minutes each day for two more weeks.

"Often, your fear thoughts will have ceased within the first two weeks of using this technique. Continue to use it periodically even after the thoughts are no longer upsetting. If the thoughts reappear, as they sometimes do, use the technique again and you'll find it to be effective more quickly the second time."

33.
All Participants

"Let's put this awareness into the context of your own life," I said to the entire group on the second afternoon of the seminar. "We've been exploring letting go of fear and expressing unconditional love for almost two days.

"Now, let's test your awareness by exploring **conscious detachment**. The idea is to enjoy all the warmth, joy and happiness that life has to offer but to detach from the negativity and allow it to flow through you without affecting you. In detaching from fear-based emotions, you let go of the fears that repress you and keep you from being all you are capable of being.

"Let's play a game called **What Would You Do If?** I'm going to share some common life situations with you, and I'd like you to tell me how you would respond to each situation with **conscious detachment** and **unconditional love.** And remember: It is always all right to be assertive but not aggressive. Assertiveness is standing up for your own human rights; aggressiveness is stepping on another's human rights. There is always a way to be assertive when necessary and to respond with unconditional love. Also, as you process yourself regarding each situation, make sure that you do not act in a way that causes you to lose self-esteem. High self-esteem is critical to your happiness. Never act in any way that causes you to lose self-esteem.

"Okay, here's the first situation: **Your married best friend boasts to you that he/she is having an affair.** How would you respond?"

Maureen: "Before this seminar, I'd probably have responded with a lot of judgment, but I would still have questioned her about all the juicy details. In the end, I would have chosen sides, my friend against her husband. But I really don't think I'd act that way now. I'd probably tell her that from my perspective of karma, she is testing herself. When she offered excuses about why she was doing what she was doing, I'd explain to her that people always act **emotionally**. They always do what they want to do and then come up with excuses to rationalize their actions. Instead of excuses, I'd suggest that she explore the fears behind her need to have an affair and attempt to get her to take responsibility for her actions. Maybe I could help process her through the four questions. But, in the end, I would accept that my friend was having an affair and that's what is. I'd tell her, 'I don't support what you are doing, but I love you and I'll be here for you.'"

Denise: "I've been through this one with two friends, so I know I didn't respond in very self-actualized ways in the past. Today, I'd support my friend as a friend, without supporting what she was doing, and as Maureen said, without taking sides. At the beginning of an affair, people are obsessed with it and feel like they can't let go. So I'd share some of the thought-stopping techniques we've learned in here. I'd stress that she had the power and ability to take control of her life if she wanted. And, if she didn't, to stop fooling herself about her real goals."

Alan: "Well, I know from personal experience how much guilt is involved, so I would help my friend explore the guilt, and I'd attempt to get him to clarify his intent in regard to his marriage. I guess what you said about being willing to make immediate sacrifices for the sake of long-term satisfactions and gains really stuck with me."

Helga: "I can't disagree with anything the others have

116

said, but I'd want my friend to understand how the mind works. First, that every time she gives in to her desire for the other man, her mind is programmed by the initial reinforcement and it will tend to increase that behavior. An awareness that thoughts are things and they create our reality would also serve her, if she was willing to accept it. I'd want her to know that she was lowering her self-esteem in doing something that resulted in guilt. High self-esteem is critical to our well being and our happiness."

Allison: "All my friends accept reincarnation, so I'd want her to explore her actions from a karmic perspective of harmony and disharmony. I know the passion of an affair would probably override logical and even spiritual considerations, but it would be important to get her to face the full implications."

"Let's move on to another situation," I said. "This time, **your mate comes home and yells at you about something unimportant.**"

Ian: "My natural reaction is to respond to aggressiveness with even more intense aggressiveness. But I have to face that it has never worked in the past and it will never do anything but make the problem worse. It would be a real test for me, but I'd tell myself that my wife was afraid and her actions were really a request for love. I'd also remind myself that whatever someone else says or does, short of physical violence, does not affect me. Only what I think about what they say or do affects me."

Tammy: "I'd remind myself that my expectations were in conflict with what is. I expected my husband to come home cheerful and glad to see me. Instead, for reasons unknown to me, that's not what is. I'd also attempt to detach from his actions. It is foolish to take someone else's reactions to you personally, good or bad, because they result from the other person's programming. Their viewpoint has nothing to do with me. The

117

way my husband related to me at that moment, in his anger, he would relate to anyone who represented to him what I represent. If his wife was named Mary instead of Tammy, and she had black hair instead of blond, he would have yelled at her just as he did with me. So, there was nothing personal in it. It's just what he does in response to particular experiences."

Lee: "I'd try to be strong enough to remind myself that other's reactions to me are nothing but statements of their viewpoint. And that has nothing to do with what actually is, so to take it seriously would be ill-advised."

Caroline: "My reaction would be to say, 'I'm sorry you're having a hard time, and I'm available to listen if you want to share anything with me.'"

"All right, let's move on to another situation," I said. **"Let's pretend that it is tomorrow and you go home and talk to your mate about this seminar, and you discuss aliveness—enjoyment in your experiences, that blood-pumping exhilaration that makes you feel glad to be alive. Remember, it's the challenge and joy and stimulation and pleasure that make life worth living. And let's say that your mate tells you that he/she doesn't think there is much aliveness or challenge in your relationship.** How would you respond?"

Elizabeth: "I'd initiate a discussion to explore potential stimulating activities that we could share together. I guess the question I'd be asking him and myself is what could we do together that would be fun and also be growth-oriented."

Cheryl: "At first, I'd probably be crushed, but I would also recognize the critical importance of dealing with the issue. I'm pretty easy-going and enjoy just about everything, so I'd begin by exploring what my husband most enjoys. Business is really his sport and hobby. He loves it, so I don't think I'm going to wait for this to come up. I'm going to explore how we could attend related seminars, conferences and trade shows. If I encouraged it, he'd take the time and these gatherings are often in different cities I'd like to visit anyway. All these activities are listed in his trade magazines."

Lori: "Well, I'd probably go out of my way to spice up our sex life, which is a great idea anyway. I won't go into details, but a little imagination can go a long way in the bedroom."

Kennedy: "I think the first thing I'd do is get my wife to talk to me about it. That would mean really listening to hear what she is saying. This would have to be done with conscious detachment, because the moment I got defensive, I'd start losing the game. I know I can't change her but I can change myself. My relationship is the most important thing in my life, so it is certainly worth some self-sacrifice which only serves me in the long run."

In the seminar room, in an altered state, or as a group discussion, I continue to ask the participants more and more difficult questions. By exploring the situations, they put their self-actualized awareness to the test, thus "setting" it into their minds for future use. The following are some situations you can use to explore your own responses:

• You are waiting to be seated in a nice restaurant. You have reservations. While you are standing there waiting for the hostess to get organized, another couple comes in. The hostess seats them first. How would you respond?

• You and another patient are seated in the waiting room of your dentist's office. The other patient sees that you are wearing a metaphysical necklace. Since he is a Born-Again Christian, he begins to tell you that you are involved with evil things and must convert and become Born-Again immediately. He is relentless and determined, raising his voice and becoming very demanding. How would you respond?

119

• One of the people you work with comes up to you and says, "I'm really sick and tired of the way you operate around here. Why don't you go get another job?" How would you respond?

• You are attending a party with a lot of friends. While you are waiting to use the bathroom, you overhear two of your friends talking about you. One is saying that she doesn't believe how boring you've become. The other agrees. How would you respond?

• You pick up your car from the garage where it is being repaired. The mechanic charged you $43.50 to fix the water pump. But, by the time you get home, the engine is overheating again. You take the car back to the mechanic, but he refuses to do anything about it. He claims it was fixed when you left his garage. How would you respond?

• You receive a letter in the mail from your son or daughter. The letter says that he or she has joined a religious cult in the Tennessee mountains and they won't be able to see you again until your next life together. How would you respond?

• There are two houses for sale in your neighborhood—one next door and the other right across the street. Both have just been sold to members of another race. How would you respond?

34.
Latham

"I feel like I've been set-up for two days," Latham said, almost humorously. One hand rested assertively on his hip while the other tugged at his mouth. "A psychic told me that this is my last life. From the way I've been approaching my life, based on what I've learned here, I don't think so. I get that I've got a lot to learn and instead of working on the basics, I've been hiding in ... in ...

dramatic demonstrations of what I've perceived to be spiritual."

"Sometimes the dramatics, or 'special effects' as I call them, get our attention, Latham," I replied. "That's how I got interested in metaphysics. But you have to ask yourself if there is any real value in what you are observing. If it doesn't change your life in positive ways, you're probably wasting your time."

"Yeah, well, once a week I go to channeling sessions at a local metaphysical center in Los Angeles," Latham continued. "A discarnate spirit speaks to us through the vocal cords of our teacher and this spirit tells us all kinds of interesting things about how the earth was created and how things work on the other side in the spiritual realms."

"I think a valid channel can provide us with beautiful, useful information," I responded. "Jane Roberts and Seth are a perfect example. But there is a channeling craze going on in this country right now and a lot of people are paying a lot of money to listen to funny voices say a lot about nothing."

"Well, I can see that I've been looking outside myself for answers and things to believe in," Latham said softly. "Because the spirit was dead, that made him magic somehow. And I've been accepting his answers about what is rather than finding my own answers."

"Latham, I once had a discarnate entity tell me, 'Dying doesn't increase your intelligence.' He went on to explain that he had a little more awareness of the relationship of non-physical to physical, but he certainly didn't have the wisdom of the universe. His perspective of what is could be very misleading. There are thousands of metaphysical books, organizations, psychics and channels, and very few agree on anything but karma and reincarnation. One can't be right and all the rest wrong. Each sees reality from his viewpoint because the viewpoint comes from his experiences. It relates to him but that doesn't mean it relates to you or will ever relate to you. A Master of Life doesn't give away his power to others."

35.
Marla

"I agree with Latham," Marla said. "I've been viewing metaphysical spirituality as something that made me superior in awareness, but I've been doing very little about evolving."

"You've been learning, you just haven't been doing much to increase your vibrational rate," I interjected.

"I don't understand," she said.

"Well, think back to the beginning of the seminar when I talked about matter being energy. Everything is vibrational energy. And you were born with a vibrational rate earned as a result of how you lived your past. Now, how you are living your present life will either increase or decrease the vibrational rate of your soul. Everything you think, say and do, and the motive, intent and desire behind everything you think, say and do, creates harmonious vibrations or disharmonious vibrations."

"You mean that if I increase my vibrational rate during this life, when I die I might find myself on a higher level on the other side?" Marla asked.

"If that's how it works," I said. "But let's assume that there are seven levels on the other side. Maybe you were on the third level before you were born. Now, because you've increased your vibrational rate, at death you'll find yourself crossing over into the fourth level. You wouldn't want to go back to the third level for it would now be much less desirable. You might like to move up to the fifth level but you'd be unable to tolerate the more intense vibrations at that level. So your level of awareness, which is another way of saying vibrational rate, dictates you will be on the fourth level."

"And the seventh level would be the Godhead, or God level?" she asked.

"For the sake of communication," I replied.

She seemed to think for a long time, and then asked, "What if I really learn all these things and my husband doesn't? I mean, what if I learn to handle our relationship with unconditional love but he just continues to be the spiteful person that he is? Would I have to come back with him in my next life?"

"Are you becoming inspired to reach the next level before he does?" I laughed. She didn't answer but made a funny face in agreement. "Well, if you learn and he doesn't, Marla, I think in the next life he'll have to find someone else with a karmic configuration that matches his own. Someone who needs to learn through the interaction he can offer and vice versa. And you'll go on to other learning."

"But when I get to the sixth or seventh levels, I won't have to come back again, will I?" she asked.

"I doubt it," I said, imitating the funny face she was making.

36.
Glenna

"Everyone in this room is seeking some kind of change," Glenna said. She was a very friendly woman, probably in her early sixties. "We all want change. John here is looking for monetary success." She pointed to another participant sitting across the aisle. "I've spoken with several people who say they want happiness and a few others want an end to the misery of bad relationships. And I know some of these people, like me, want to evolve spiritually, but that is still change. Are you advocating one simple set of guidelines to generate all these changes?"

"There are three ways to create change in a human being, Glenna," I responded. "The first way is adding something, such as people, things, environment, programming, awareness, or challenge. The second way is taking something away, such as people, things, environment, etc. And the third way is getting someone to be his or her True Self. That is primarily what we've been working on in here. This is transcendental change. You peel away all your fears to find that beneath them you are already a Master of Life, a fully self-actualized soul, capable of expressing unconditional love in response to every situation you encounter in your life. From this level of True Self, you will have transcended your current limited viewpoints of success, happiness, relationships, and everything else. I see this as being in the world but not of it."

*The fish trap exists
because of the fish, and
once you've caught the
fish, you can forget
about the trap.
The rabbit snare exists
because of the rabbit,
and once you've captured
the rabbit, you can
forget about the snare.
Words exist because
of their meaning, and
once you have the
meaning, you can forget
about the words.*

37.
Mastering Relationships

To love and be loved is the deepest psychological need in human beings. In the ideal relationship, both partners maintain their integrity and individuality while—through their union—increasing the potential to become all they are capable of being.

My wife Tara and I developed 12 **Master of Life** tenets we feel support and strengthen a good relationship, and which can help to repair a problem relationship.

LOVE

Love each other as you would be loved, cherishing the passion and joy, while allowing the negativity to flow through you without affecting you.

ACCEPTANCE

Treasure each other's uniqueness and accept each other as you are without expectations of change.

COMMITMENT

Totally commit to your relationship—mentally, physically, spiritually, emotionally and financially. Withholding reflects doubts that will undermine the foundation of your union.

SUPPORT

Support each other in ways that increase self-esteem. This is critical to a good relationship, for to love another you must love yourself.

DETACHMENT

Let the little things go. Before reacting negatively, ask yourself, "Does it really matter or am I just acting out of a need to be right?"

COMMUNICATION

Openly communicate and share yourself. The greatest gift you can give each other is to be all of who you are. Be willing to discuss needs and compromise solutions.

LISTEN

Listen to each other and be willing to appreciate the other's position even when you don't agree. Also, learn to hear what isn't being verbalized.

COMFORT

Provide comfort to each other in the midst of worldly concerns. Be friends as well as lovers and let your union be a refuge of balance and harmony.

TRANSCEND ANGER

Rise above anger by saying to yourself, "I am angry because I had expectations of gaining approval or control in this situation. These are not my rights."

TIME

Always make time for each other and find fulfillment in the current moment. Shared activities are the building blocks of a good relationship.

TRANSCEND BLAME

Blame is an expression of self-pity and is incompatible with the acceptance of karma. Everything is karmic, so the situation was self-created to test your level of awareness.

SPIRITUALITY

Encourage each other to evolve spiritually. Through faith, you can transcend the darkness and attain peace of mind.

Master of Life Seminar Trainings are based upon logic, contemporary psychotherapies, the latest brain/mind research, Zen and metaphysics. Dick Sutphen offers the awareness as a New Age philosophy/religion of self that you don't join ... you live. Readers of Dick's books have often asked, "Why should I attend a seminar when I can get a lot of the concepts from his books?"

It is a difficult question to answer if you haven't attended a Sutphen Seminar. Dick calls the seminars "a process of liberation." The experience and interaction between Sutphen and the participants creates a synergistic energy that generates insight.

The fast pacing of the short talks, altered-state sessions, sharing, group mills, and processing encounters like those in this book, conditions you to accept awareness. This awareness is then used to build more awareness which serves as the foundation for major breakthroughs that remove the blocks keeping you from experiencing your potential. And you always use your own experiences as the basis of your acceptance. Dick often says to the participants, "I don't have your answers—only you have your answers—but I know how to help you find them."

Sutphen Seminars are conducted in approximately 24 cities per year, usually on weekends. Sedona, Arizona, the site of the energy vortexes, is the location for three psychic development seminars each year, and several specialized five-day trainings are usually offered in the Los Angeles area.

You can write for complete information and a sample copy of *Master of Life Magazine*. It is published quarterly and sent free to anyone attending a seminar or purchasing **Valley of the Sun** books or tapes. Each issue contains many exciting feature articles that relate to Master of Life concepts of self-help and self-responsibility, and also includes a listing of 300 Sutphen tapes: hypnosis, meditation, sleep programming, subliminal programming, symbol therapy, children's programming and a growing line of New Age music albums by some of the finest artists in the country. Write: Sutphen Corporation, Box 38, Malibu, California 90265.

About The Author

Dick Sutphen is the author of 36 books, a seminar trainer and an innovative hypnotist who specializes in regressive techniques and reprogramming. He developed the group exploration techniques now being used internationally. In addition to his twice-yearly spiritual potential seminars, Dick conducts a professional teaching seminar for psychologists, psychiatrists and medical practitioners in addition to New Age individuals who desire to learn hypnosis and trainer techniques.

Dick's bestselling books include **You Were Born Again To Be Together, Unseen Influences** and **Past Lives, Future Loves** (Simon Schuster Pocket Books). Dick has produced hundreds of hypnosis tapes and he has appeared on most of the national television talk shows and on more than 350 local radio and television shows.

Sutphen is also president of **Reincarnationists, Inc.,** a nonprofit, tax-exempt organization with the goal of "peaceful planetary transformation through the mass communication of the liberating, self-responsible concepts of reincarnation and karma."

Dick lives with his wife, Tara, in Malibu, California, where he writes and directs corporate activities.